I0535509

JAX JILLIAN

Ryan's Letters

PRAISE FOR JAX JILLIAN'S DEBUT NOVEL *LARKIN'S LETTERS*

"It is an absolutely elegantly written story. This exquisitely written debut novel is one you should not pass up." – *Drue Hoffman, DRC Promotions*

"This book was phenomenal, and probably one of the best of this genre I have read in a long time" – *Kayla West, Journey with Books*

"*Larkin's Letters* is a must-read and should be on every person's reading list." – *Teri Lloyd, Sportochick's Musings*

"There are no words to say how much this book touched me. Great job and I look forward to reading more stories from this author." – *Deborah Bean, DRC Promotions Review Team*

"This superbly written debut novel is one you should not pass up, even with the sadness it makes you feel." – *Lynn Barret, Sassy Southern Book Affair*

"The author's skill at reaching my emotions and keeping me engaged guarantees I will pick up the next book I find with Jax Jillian's name." – *Laura Roth, Laura's Interests*

DEDICATION

To those who have loved, lost, and found the strength to love again

To my GNO ladies – Kristen, Gem, Jinky, Sonya, Kathy, Jennifer, and Lynn – thank you for your humor, support, and acceptance. You have been everything I need whenever I have needed it.

CHAPTER 1

Looking back.

That's what Ryan Boone found himself doing since his wife's death. Looking back at their time together every day. Looking back at all the letters she had left behind. He had been going through the motions of moving forward, making everybody around him think he was okay, but he wasn't. He couldn't stop looking back.

Today, he found himself looking down into the waters of the Great Egg Harbor Bay, watching the ripples in the water move back and forth as his boat rocked slowly against the current. He was watching his reflection bounce up and down in rhythm with the rocking of the boat as it started to become blurry before slowly disappearing. Finally, all he could see was nothing. Complete darkness ensued.

"Don't give up." Her voice echoed off the salt water that was slowly filling his lungs. "Ryan, open your eyes. Open your eyes, Ryan." That voice.

He knew that voice.

Larkin.

Could it really be her? His eyes shot open, and he saw her blue eyes glaring at him through the foggy salt water that was swallowing his body. The rip current was fiercely pulling his legs down toward the bottom of the bay, but he could feel her fighting to keep him afloat. "Stay with me, Ryan." Her hands cupped his face, and he could see the worry in her eyes. "Please, don't give up," she pleaded. He pulled her hands away from his face and held them tight in his. He hadn't seen her since that night on the beach, the night he spread her ashes, and he was not going to let go of her this time. He held onto her as tight as he could while they kicked up toward the surface. He could see the sun's rays slice through the ocean's layers as he got closer to the top. As his head broke through the water's surface, he could feel her grasp diminish. He spun his battered body around and around, panicked, not exactly sure as to what just happened. Almost drowning had left him confused and disoriented. There was one thing he was sure of. She was there. He saw her. He felt her, but now she was gone. He had tried so hard to hold onto her, but she had slipped away again.

Dear Blue Eyes,

In your letters, you wrote to me that time heals what reason cannot. There was and never will be a reason why you were taken from me, a reason why your life was ended so short. I wish you could have told me how much time because I feel like there will never be enough time for me to completely heal.

I still look for you. I long to see your blue eyes among the stars as they decorate the night sky. I long to see your smile among the waves as they crash against the grains of sand at my feet. I long to hear your voice, my lullaby, among the crackling of the flames that burn from the bonfire as I sit here writing to you.

It has been eight months since you have been taken from me, and I haven't written to you since I finished reading your letters. But something happened to me today, and I don't know how else to deal with it except to write to you. I took the boat out on the back bays to fish early this morning where nobody else was around, and all I could think about was dying. Not about wanting to die but about all the different ways someone can die. For me, I think drowning would be one of the worst ways to die—gasping for air as your lungs slowly fill with water, your body being pulled under by the unforgiving rip currents. Even so, it's how I would want to go. I grew up surrounded by the ocean. Most of my childhood was spent in the water. I am at peace on the water. I spread your ashes over the water. It's where you are, so it's where I want to be.

As I was waiting for the fish to bite, I saw your reflection on the water. I couldn't help but feel you were calling for me, needing me. Before I knew it, I felt myself jump into the water not your reflection. I felt the rip current pull me down, and you know I know how to swim against the rip current, but I didn't try. I just let the current take me into your reflection, but then I saw you. I felt you. I don't know why I keep thinking you still need me. I saw you that night on the beach, the night I spread your ashes. You were happy. You were safe. You were healthy. I know you do not need me anymore. I thought I was trying to save you by jumping into the water, but I now realize that all along you were trying to save ME.

My dearest Larkin.

Help me.

I'm drowning.

Ryan Boone sat on his private beach that sat behind the house he and his wife, Larkin, had shared in Longport, New Jersey. It was a warm Sunday evening in late July, and he could see the lights emanate off the Ferris wheel just across the inlet on Ocean City's boardwalk. Summer was in full swing, and the warm air was still haunted by Larkin's absence. It had only been eight months since her death, and he still missed her so much. She was gone, and all he had were her letters. He read one every morning, but he still hadn't seen her ghost since the night he spread her ashes. Well, that was until he saw her this past morning. Ryan gently folded the letter in half and penned her name across the top. He stared at it for a moment before brushing his lips across her name. Hesitating for just a moment, he slowly guided the letter to the bonfire's flames that shot up into the night sky. He figured the ocean breeze would take the letter's ashes into the atmosphere, just like that night four months ago when he spread her ashes. It was the only way he could think of getting her the letter. Maybe, just maybe, he desperately thought.

Ryan sat under the moonlight for hours, watching for any jerk that his fishing rod might make. Night fishing had become a passion of his since Larkin had passed. He would sit on the beach for hours, the end of the rod set up in the sand next to his chair, and he would read, studying his lines. He was filming a movie in Philadelphia during the week, his first since almost two years ago. It wasn't easy for him to go back, but his best friend, Sarah Madison, was filming with him, and she definitely helped make his transition back to work much easier. But tonight, he wasn't able to focus on his lines. All he could think about was almost drowning earlier that day. He couldn't help but ask himself if he was really trying to save Larkin, or was he perhaps trying to drown. The latter was unfathomable. Or was it? There was no way he would even think about taking his life. He realized just how precious life was when Larkin got sick. He could only imagine what Larkin would think if she knew he would try to end his. He had promised her he would keep living, but he felt it was getting harder and harder to do that. He didn't realize how alone he would feel. Even when he was surrounded by his friends and his family, he still felt so alone.

The screaming of the seagulls above had startled Ryan out of his sleep. He had fallen asleep in his beach chair as the flames extinguished into the night sky. He quickly looked at his watch and with a panic, gathered his things, grabbed the fishing rod, and headed inside. He was late. He needed to be in Philadelphia in an hour, and with traffic, he knew it was going to take him at least two to get there. As he packed for the week, he texted Sarah to let her know he overslept. Yeah, he was late, but he was also the lead producer of the movie, so he wasn't worried too much about the repercussions. Ryan secured the house, threw his luggage on his back, and jumped on his Triumph motorcycle, his latest impulsive purchase. After he bought the motorcycle, his mother had expressed her concerns that he was becoming reckless, but it had nothing to do with that. He felt free when he was on the bike, just like when he was on his boat. Sometimes he would find himself daydreaming that Larkin was sitting behind him with her arms wrapped around his waist. He imagined they were driving across the country together, leaving everything behind and heading nowhere specific, following the road to wherever it took them. It didn't matter where, just as long as they were together.

After the two-hour ride, Ryan pulled up to the set and parked his Triumph next to his trailer. He got settled before heading to makeup, went over his lines for the scene he was about to film, then met with the director. He felt like a zombie as he journeyed through the day, and there were many times he wasn't able to get the scene right, whether it was because he forgot his lines or the director just wasn't getting what he wanted from Ryan. It got so bad that before pulling him aside, Sarah yelled, "Cut!"

"Are you okay, Ryan?" she asked.

"Yeah, I am just tired, so I can't concentrate. I didn't get much sleep last night."

"Are you sure that's it?" Sarah pressed.

He knew she was worried about him. She worried about how he was still dealing with Larkin's death. There was no way he was going to tell her about the near-drowning incident. Then she would never leave him alone.

"Yes, Sarah. That's it. I'm just tired."

Sarah reached for Ryan's hand and squeezed it tight. She always grabbed his hand when she knew he was hurting. She always knew. It's like she could read his mind. He hated it, but even so, he was thankful for it. There were many afternoons on his back deck when they would sit hand-in-hand, quietly, for as long as he needed. Sarah's silence was everything he needed. She never judged; she never pushed him. She would just listen whenever he did talk, and she would just hold his hand. It always made him feel better. But this time, he didn't want to talk. He just sat in silence next to her for a while before deciding to call it a day. He figured he would go back to his trailer and get some rest. Last night's sleep—if that's what you wanted to call it—on the beach chair was not the best rest he could have gotten. But deep down, he knew that wasn't the reason he couldn't concentrate. Larkin was the reason. Seeing and touching her yesterday was haunting him. Why did her ghost come back? It had been four months. Why now? What did she want? What was she trying to tell him? All of these questions just swirled around and around in his head. He needed to find the answers, but he had no idea how.

Ryan laid on the couch in his trailer and closed his eyes, hoping he would nod off into a deep sleep. There was so much noise coming from the set traffic just outside the trailer, but he had grown accustomed to falling asleep surrounded by noise. Ever since Larkin died, he would fall asleep every night listening to her favorite Frank Sinatra CD—the one with their wedding song—or to the television. Even the seagulls that would dance and sing outside his bedroom window along with the crashing of the waves had become his favorite lullaby. He found that the quieter it was, the harder it was for him to fall asleep.

Just as Ryan was starting to finally drift off, a dream of what happened yesterday morning in the bay startled him almost right off the couch. He didn't know what to do to forget it. It had been haunting him ever since it happened. He needed to see her again. He needed to know that everything was okay. Was everything okay? If it was, why was she back? He felt like he needed to talk to somebody about what had happened, but he didn't know who. If he said anything to Sarah, or his other best friends, Ian and Justin, they would just worry about him. He didn't need that. The only person he knew he needed to talk to was Larkin. But how? He still felt like he had so much to say to her, so he decided to write her another letter. It was the only way he could think of to talk to her. The letters she had left him were her way of talking to him after she died. He could only hope that somehow she could hear him. That somehow she was listening. He had a feeling she was.

He scrambled to find some paper and a pen. Thankfully, he had a notebook he had been taking notes in about the film production.

My Larkin,

I wrote to you last night. Did you get it?

There is so much going on in my head right now. I need you to be here. I need to talk to you. But then again, if you were here, everything would be okay. I don't know how else to talk to you but to write to you. I have a feeling that somehow you will be able to read this. I don't know how, but you're an angel now, so anything is possible, right? You were always an angel in my eyes.

I made good on my promise to you. I went back to work. It took me a while, but I found my way with a little help from you and your letters, of course. Sarah and I are working on a film together. You may have heard of it. It's called "Jillian's

Touch". That's right, Lark. I finished your screenplay. I can't believe you started writing it, and I didn't even know it. Oh, and I got the novel published, too, so you are officially a published author. Congratulations! I donate all of your profits to the American Cancer Society in your name. I am doing everything I can to honor your memory. You never got the chance to finish reading me the entire novel, but I finished it on my own as I was completing the screenplay. I never got the chance to tell you how amazing I think it is. You were such a talented writer, Lark. It's a shame the world will never get to read anymore of your beautiful writing.

We are filming in Philadelphia, your favorite city. It's also close to Longport, so I can come home on the weekends to be close to you. Sarah, Ian, and Justin come to see me often. They miss you. Justin doesn't get to come as often as Sarah or Ian because he is filming a movie in Los Angeles.

I try to see your parents as much as I can. It is still really hard for me to go inside your house. There are so many memories of our childhood together. They are doing okay, though. I think your father is taking it a little harder than your mother, but overall they seem to be healing. I sometimes get the feeling they would like to see me more, but I think they also know it is hard for me to see them. It's my fault. I should go see them more often. I'm working on it. I'll get there, right? I have to.

I take ol' "Blue Eyes" out every weekend to fish. Did I tell you I named the boat after you? It is *the only time I feel at peace. You know me and the water. It's my favorite place. We've shared so many memories on the boat. I feel close to you when I am on it. I wish you were still here. I would trade it in for a houseboat, and you and I could sail away and live on the water for the rest of our lives. But that's not going to happen, is it?*

Larkin, I have done my best to move on with my life. I still read your letters, and they help me get through each day, but not a day goes by that I don't wish you were by my side.

I love you.

I miss you.

I still feel like I'm drowning.

It's going to get better, right?

Still yours,

Ryan

CHAPTER 2

The tired sun was sinking below the South Jersey shoreline as Ryan introduced the match head's flame to the corner of the letter he had written when he was in Philadelphia this past week. The breeze carried the letter's ashes into the night sky, and the burning embers blended in with the stars. Larkin was among the stars, he thought, and now, so was the letter he had written to her. There were times he felt like he was being foolish, writing to a dead person and thinking she was actually going to read his letters. Any normal person would think he was crazy. Maybe I am, he thought. But he found that writing to her was helping to keep his sanity.

As usual, Ryan had his fishing rod set up in the sand with the line reeled out into the inlet. He kept watch for any sudden jerks on the line, but tonight the fish didn't seem interested in biting. Ryan blamed it on the ruckus coming from the neighbor's house. It was scaring the fish away. He was actually starting to get frustrated, but he let it be. It was just for that night. He was getting new neighbors, and they had started to move in that day. He hoped they were almost finished. He couldn't take another night of all the noise. The one reason he loved Longport was because it was quiet, a far cry from Los Angeles or New York City.

Ryan decided to take a walk along the edge of the bay, just deep enough to get his ankles wet. The water was lukewarm, and he couldn't help but chuckle to himself. Well, *he* thought it was warm, but Larkin always thought the Atlantic Ocean was so cold, and he always had to carry her in to get her to go into the water with him. As they went swimming more often, she got used to it and eventually became oblivious to the cold. Every now and then, he would crouch down and look into the water, hoping to see her reflection again, but of course, he didn't. As Ryan journeyed back to his house, he could see someone in the distance sitting on the dune next to his house. It was the same dune he and Larkin would sit on to feed the seagulls. It was too dark to make out who it was, but one thing he knew for certain was that whoever it was, they didn't belong there. As he came a little closer, he yelled out to the stranger.

"Hey! That dune is private property! You can't be there!"

The stranger looked his way, but he still couldn't make out who it was. He figured it was probably one of the new neighbors, and they were probably harmless, but either way, he didn't want them on the dune.

"Do you hear me? You can't be on there!"

As he was yelling out, his other neighbor, Lou, had heard him from his back deck and called out for him.

"Everything okay, Ryan?"

Ryan gave Lou a quick glance and held up his finger before turning back to the dune, but the stranger was no longer there. It was hard to believe. He had only looked away for a split second. How could they have disappeared that fast? He examined the area as well as his house to make sure they weren't trespassing anywhere else on his property, but there was no sight of anyone. He came back outside and yelled across the back deck over to Lou, who had been standing on his deck, waiting.

"Yeah, Lou. Thanks. Everything is okay." Ryan liked Lou. He was a good man, and he had been really helpful to Ryan after Larkin died. He also keeps an eye on his house when he is away for the week.

"Hey, Lou? Have you met the new neighbors yet?"

"Nah, they just started moving in today."

"Yeah, well, I think one of them was just sitting on my dune. Can you keep an eye out during the week?"

"Yeah, sure, Ryan. You know I will."

Ryan packed up the fishing gear, extinguished the fire, and went inside. He had a big day ahead of him tomorrow. He was going to see Larkin's parents for dinner which always made him nervous. He met with them once a month, and it still wasn't easy. There were too many memories in that house, and he could still see the sorrow in their eyes. He always tried to put on a strong front so \ they couldn't see he was still grieving. Besides, he needed to take care of them. He wanted them to know they could lean on him if they needed to. He had promised Larkin he would look out for them.

My blue-eyed Larkin,

There are new neighbors moving in next door into John and Mae's old place. I haven't met them yet, well officially, that is. Last night, I was taking a walk along the beach, and when I was coming back, I saw someone sitting on the dune— you know, our dune, the one we always sat and fed the seagulls on. It was also the one I started reading your letters on. I yelled out to the person to leave, and in a flash, they were gone. It was weird. I glanced away for one second, and no sooner were they gone. I obviously spooked them, and they bolted right out of there. I guess I can't say for certain it was the new neighbor, but who else could it have been? Longport is a quiet town with little to no crime. If you were here, I know what you would say. You would say, "Maybe they just wanted to check out the view." You always gave people the benefit of the doubt. I was always the more cautious one. I think I became that way when I lived in LA. City life will do that to you. You can never be too sure, and you are always watching your back.

I went and had dinner with your parents earlier today. I see them once a month to make sure they are okay, just like I promised you, and I think they are coping well. I know they miss you tremendously. I finally told them today. I told them about your letters. I told them you had written to me throughout your sickness, and you left them behind for me to keep. I don't know why it took me so long. I guess I didn't want to upset them, although I am not quite sure why I thought they would have been upset. I thought maybe it would just fuel the grief that was still simmering in their hearts. I don't know if maybe some part of me thought they might be jealous, too. Maybe it was just me. Maybe I was too scared to talk about the letters. It did take me awhile to even read them. I still struggle with reading them. But it is getting better. I promise.

Your parents were great. They always make me feel safe. No matter how sad or scared I feel, they always sense it, and they make me feel like everything is going to be okay. They were happy you had written to me. They knew the letters would help me to grieve. They weren't surprised, either. Your dad said, "That Larkin, she always knew what you needed." He's right. You did. You knew I would need those letters, and I will always need those letters.

Love,

Ryan

Ryan sealed the letter and placed it in his safe in the bedroom closet. It was Sunday, and he was getting ready to leave for Philadelphia for the week. He didn't have time to light a fire and burn the letter. Next weekend, he thought. The sun was starting to descend behind the tired bay, and the weekend tourists were starting their journeys home. He needed to get on the road; he was to meet Sarah for dinner when he got into the city. He didn't want to keep her waiting too late.

Ryan packed his bag and checked the house to make sure everything was in its place before walking over to Lou's house to drop his key in his mailbox. He always left him an extra key during the week in case Lou needed to get in. Lou would normally never need to go into Ryan's place, but he gave him one anyway. It gave him peace of mind to know Lou was looking out. He also thought it made Lou feel important. He was a widow, and his only child lived in Florida, so Ryan figured he was probably lonely. He was a retired cop from New York City, so he was tough as well as intelligent. Ryan trusted him completely. They would go fishing together out on Ryan's boat, and Ryan loved listening to Lou's cop stories, especially the ones from 9/11. Lou was on the front lines when the towers fell, and he knew several of the cops and firefighters that were killed. He couldn't talk about it without getting teary-eyed. Lou was a good man, and his experiences when he was a cop made him who he was today—trustworthy and strong. He had lost his wife to cancer over a decade ago, so Ryan knew Lou knew how he felt, and that made Ryan appreciate him even more.

My dearest Larkin,

I keep having the same dream over and over again. I am sitting on the boat with the fishing rod perched up in the rod holder as I sit writing to you. I am in the middle of the bay, and there is no one else around. The sky looks dangerous. Red and purple clouds blanket the earth, and the water is eerily calm. I guess it is the calm before the storm. Suddenly, the water begins to wake, rocking my boat side to side. I start to hear someone screaming. Not a painful scream; more like a scream for help. I'm looking all around, but I can't see anyone. The boat is rocking harder and harder, and I can't keep my balance. At the same time, the screams are getting louder and closer. Thunder starts to shake the earth, and I can see lightning in the distance but no rain. I keep looking to find the source of the scream, but still, no one. I manage to maintain my balance, and I crawl to the edge of the boat to look into the water. And what I see in the water wakes me up from this dream every time. What I see, Larkin, is the face of a girl, but her face is blurry, and she is screaming for help. She is drowning. I think the girl is you, and just as I prepare to jump in to save you, your face suddenly appears next to hers, you grab her, and you both disappear.

I wish I could stay asleep longer so I can see what happens next. I don't quite understand why I am having this dream or what it means. Do you? I wish I knew who the blurry face is or what it signifies. Maybe the blurry face is you before you died, and your face signifies your happiness in heaven. Are you trying to tell me something, Lark? Are you trying to push me into letting you go? That you're at peace? I don't know. I feel like it means more than that. I am grasping at air right now. I have no idea what it means. I just hope I figure it out soon.

Love,

Ryan

It was a typical recovery Saturday for Ryan after filming long hours during the week. Spending the day fishing on the "Blue Eyes," grilling his catch for the day, and then burying himself in the movie script, memorizing lines for scenes he was to film in the upcoming week. He looked forward to the weekend. The movie was draining him. It was the first time he was not only acting but producing as well, so he had a lot more responsibilities than just remembering his lines and delivering them in front of a camera. But deep down, he knew it wasn't just the movie dragging him down. It was Larkin. Ever since seeing her that day on the water, he had been so distracted. Even Sarah had noticed. More than once, she had questioned him about how he was doing. She knew something wasn't right, but he hadn't told her what happened, and he doesn't know if he ever will. There were many times he had asked himself if maybe it was because he was filming Larkin's screenplay. It had made him feel so close to her, almost like she was there watching. Or maybe he was just desperate to believe she was there watching. All he knew was he was missing her more than ever at this time in his life, and he was trying to find reason, so he decided to blame the film. That was a good enough reason for him.

Darkness had started to set in over the tired bay, and the shore's exuberant tourist life had started to dwindle into a fast slumber for the evening. Ryan set up his fishing rod next to the newly ignited bonfire before getting the letter he had written Larkin last weekend. He slid it, along with this most recent one, into an envelope and performed his Saturday night ritual of "sending" it to Larkin. As the ashes melted into the atmosphere, Ryan's old friends screeched overhead, thanking him for the bread, and the wind serenaded him into a deep sleep.

For the third time this week, the same dream startled Ryan out of his sleep. He was angry at himself for not being able to stay asleep longer to see what happened next. The time on his watch signaled it was way too late for him to be sleeping on the beach. He looked around at the surrounding bay and realized the only thing keeping him company was the moon. The night air was warm, but not humid, and the only sound was that of the rippling of the waves as they crested. The fire had diminished to just a small pile of ash, and Ryan threw his half-full bottle of water on it anyway just to make sure. He gathered his things and made the sleepy walk back to the house.

As Ryan approached the bottom step of the patio stairs, a sudden movement over the dunes caught the corner of his eye. He slowly looked around but couldn't see anything. He figured it was probably just a seagull hovering over the dunes, looking for a late night snack. He paused momentarily just to be sure and after realizing it was nothing, he started back up the stairs. Ryan secured the patio furniture just in case it got windy overnight, and then headed inside. He gave one last glance out of the sliding glass door before he turned the deck light off, and just before he was about to turn the switch, he saw the stranger sitting on the dune again. He rushed back out onto the deck and screamed for him or her to leave.

"Hey! You need to get off the dune! That's private property!"

Ryan hurried down to the dune to confront the stranger, but as soon as he got there, the stranger was gone. Even though he couldn't see the stranger, Ryan still yelled out in hopes that whoever it was, the stranger was still close enough to hear.

"Stay off the dunes! You hear me? Stay off my property!"

It had to be the neighbor, he thought. It had to be. He wasn't having this problem until the night they moved in. Ryan looked over at the new neighbor's house, and it was completely dark, except for a few window candles. He decided he was going to stop by tomorrow and confront them about their trespassing on his property. He would do it politely though. After all, he was a reasonable man. Larkin would have made sure he would give them the benefit of the doubt, and he would. Maybe they thought the dunes were public property, even though they were obviously on his. He would do his best to be polite, but the dunes were sacred to him, and he didn't want anyone on them. Period.

CHAPTER 3

It was a sunny and comfortably warm Sunday afternoon, and Lux Johnston stood at the edge of her back deck, clutching her cup of tea while leaning slightly forward over the cherry-stained wooden railing as her blonde hair blew amongst the ocean breeze. She was trying, but she couldn't get a good enough look at her next-door neighbor who had been washing his boat since he docked thirty minutes ago. She wasn't trying to be nosy. She was just mostly curious about the neighbor she had just moved in next to. She had been sitting on her back deck when she saw him the night before sitting by a bonfire with a fishing rod planted next to him in the sand. She had noticed him throw what looked like an envelope into the flames before studying the night sky for a while as the embers blew in the breeze. Even though she was a property away from him, she could sense he was sad. She didn't know why she sensed that. She just did.

As Lux watched her neighbor hose down his boat, she couldn't help but notice how handsome he was. He seemed to be about her age, but she couldn't be too sure. One thing she was for sure of was that he lived alone, and he wasn't around during the week. She had only moved to Longport one week ago, and she had attempted to knock on his door a couple of times during the past week to introduce herself, but no one ever answered. It wasn't until Friday when she bumped into the other neighbor, Lou, and he informed her that he worked out of town during the week. He would be home that evening for the weekend. She had wanted to make it a point to meet him over the weekend, but she had to work all day yesterday, and he had been on his boat all day today. She figured now was as good a time as any, so she grabbed the tray of brownies she had baked earlier that morning and nervously made her way across the beach to her neighbor's dock.

"Excuse me?" Lux awkwardly offered as she approached him. She didn't know why she felt so nervous to meet him.

Her presence caught the corner of his eye, and he quickly shut off the hose to acknowledge her.

"Can I help you?"

"Hi. I wanted to introduce myself. I'm your new neighbor." She held out the tray of brownies as she greeted him

"Oh, so *you're* my new neighbor?" She was

taken aback by the accusing tone of his voice, but she shrugged it off as her just being nervous.

"Yeah, that's me. I'm Lux."

He turned the hose back on and resumed rinsing off the boat. "Lux? That's an interesting name," he responded, without even giving her a glance.

"Yeah, I get that all of the time." She paused for a moment waiting for some sort of response, but he just went about his business of cleaning the boat. "I'm new to the area. I moved here from Massachusetts." She suddenly realized she was still holding out the tray of brownies, so she set them on the edge of the dock. She was stunned by the way he was dismissing her. He wouldn't make eye contact with her, and it was almost as if he was ignoring her by the way he just continued to wash the boat as she talked to him. She again waited for him to introduce himself to her, but when she realized he wasn't interested in talking, she decided it was time for her to go.

"Well, it was nice meeting you," she said.

As she started to walk away, she heard the water stop spraying against the boat and heard him call out to her.

"Hey, welcome to Longport," he said, "but stay off my dunes. Next time I see you on them, I'll call the police and report you for trespassing."

She was confused by what he had just said to her. She had no idea what he was talking about.

She had never been on his dunes before.

"I'm sorry, I don't know what you're talking about."

"Last weekend, I saw you sitting on my dunes the night you were moving in. I called out to you, and you disappeared. I saw you last night, too. They are not public property."

"You must have me confused with someone else. That wasn't me." She suddenly felt angry that she had to defend herself from his accusation. He was a real jerk, she thought. She was sorry she ever came over to meet him.

"Well, it wasn't any of my other neighbors."

"Well, maybe it was a tourist," she said with resentment.

"No, tourists don't usually come to this end of the island. It's all residential."

Lux was becoming angrier as the conversation continued. "Well, whatever. It wasn't me. I am sorry you think it was, but it wasn't. Anyway, I am sorry I bothered you. Have a nice life...on your dunes...or wherever." She stumbled over her words.

She took several steps away from the dock before she realized she had left the brownies on the dock. She hesitantly walked back over and grabbed the tray, making sure not to make eye contact with him, and quickly walked away. He certainly didn't deserve any brownies, she thought. As Lux walked back to her house, she was upset about the encounter she just had with her neighbor. She was new to the area, and she was hoping to make some friends outside of the new friends she was making at work. She could only hope his attitude and actions were not indicative of Longport as a whole. She prayed she didn't make a bad decision coming here. She had moved here to get a new start, and she certainly wasn't off to a good one.

Hey Larkin,

I miss you. I find myself looking for you in every shadow, in every raindrop, in every ray of sun. I look for your smile amongst the clouds, and I look for your eyes amongst the stars. Every corner I turn, I pray you will be standing there. I thought it was supposed to get better, but ever since I saw you that morning in the bay, I feel it is getting worse.

I am taking a break from filming right now. We are behind in schedule a little bit, so everyone is working hard. I am trying to get some rest before we resume, but you know me, I can never sleep, especially during the day. We have about another month of filming left, and it has been harder than I thought. Every scene I film, I know I am saying the words you wrote, and it is tearing me up. I wish you were here to see your screenplay, our screenplay, come to fruition. It's good, Lark. It's really good. I should be excited about it, but it's hard when I can't be excited with you. I just hope I have the strength to finish it.

It's the start of August, and summer is starting to wind down. I remember last August like it was yesterday. We were newlyweds, and you were healthy. It's amazing how life can change in an instant. Just one year ago, we were safe in each other's arms, and now, you're gone. I am no longer safe.

Love, Ry.

Ryan stood sipping his coffee as he watched the rain pound against the sliding glass door. He was waiting patiently for it to stop so he could sit on the beach and burn the letter he had written to Larkin this past week. He couldn't understand why he felt so strongly about having to "send" the letters to her. He was sure she could read them. He didn't know how, but something inside of him told him she could. Well, it was more like he *hoped* she could. But all he was surviving on right now was hope, so he held onto it as tight as he could.

The shatter of the coffee mug against the hardwood floor startled Ryan out of his sleep. He had fallen asleep on the couch, mug in hand, and television playing. He quickly cleaned up the glass and the spilled coffee before looking outside again to check the weather. The rain had finally stopped, but the wind was battering the waves, and the sand was dancing on top of the beach. Ryan checked his watch. It was late, 11:17 p.m. to be exact, but he didn't care. He was going to burn the letter no matter what time it was.

It was too windy to start a bonfire, so Ryan just clutched the letter with a grill tong and lit it with a match. The only thing the wind was good for was whisking the embers into the night sky. He sat on his beach chair and watched as the letter slowly melted into nothing, and again, he found himself looking for Larkin among the waves.

Ryan slowly headed back to the house, and on the way, he stopped to arrange the scattered patio furniture pillows back into their proper places. Before going inside, he rested his elbows on the deck railing and scanned the horizon with his tired eyes. He always thought the ocean's most peaceful time was at night. It too was at rest. No speeding boats to disrupt the calm waters, no fishing rods poking at its hungry guests. He gave the horizon one last glance before the corner of his eye was caught by a silhouette sitting on his dune. Frustration and anger set in as he had already warned her not to go on his dunes again. As he hurried toward the dunes, he yelled out.

"Hey, what did I tell you last week? You can't be on my dunes!"

She didn't move away this time. She continued to sit there as he got closer.

"Hey? Do you hear me? You need to leave!"

No sooner than when that last word escaped his lips, he became suddenly speechless. He was close enough to make eye contact with her, and he would recognize those eyes anywhere.

"Larkin?"

"Hi, beautiful-faced boy." Her smile was

finally among the clouds, her eyes among the stars. "I got your letters."

He approached her, hesitantly, afraid she would vanish as he got closer. "You did?"

She nodded. "They're beautiful."

"Just like you," he quickly responded. He continued to creep closer toward her, still not sure if he should believe she was actually there. He finally found himself sitting next to her, and he reached his hand out slowly to touch her face. As his fingertips grazed her cheek, she reached up and grabbed his hand and interlaced her fingers with his. She was dressed in an all-white lace dress, and her eyes were as blue as the ocean. Her presence was angelic, and her touch was so gentle.

She was real; he could feel her. She had finally come back. "You're really here. I can't believe you're here." Her smile took his pain away.

"I miss you, Lark."

"I'm proud of you, Ryan."

"Why?"

"I'm proud of your strength. You are moving forward, living your life. You went back to work."

"I don't feel like I am living. I don't feel like I am moving forward. I feel so alone."

"You're not alone, Ryan. Trust me."

"I do."

"Do me one favor? Leave your heart open. Can you do that for me?"

Ryan studied her face, trying to understand why she was asking him that.

"Ryan? Promise me you will keep your heart open."

"Okay," he hesitantly responded. "Okay, I will."

Larkin reached out and cupped Ryan's face into her hands. "Thank you for the letters. Now, close your eyes."

"Larkin, no, please don't leave."

"Close your eyes, beautiful boy. I promise you I won't leave you alone. I'll be here when you need me."

Ryan reluctantly closed his eyes, and as he did, he could feel the tears building up behind them. He tried to grab Larkin's hands when he felt them slip away from his face, but all he could grab was air. She was gone. As he opened his eyes, a single tear escaped the back of his eyelid and trickled down his face.

My beautiful Larkin,

My encounter with you last evening kept me up all night. I kept pacing back and forth from the bed to the bedroom balcony to see if you had come back to the dune. My mind raced back and forth between what was real and what I thought was real. You are gone. I know this. Was I dreaming? There was no way I was dreaming. When I do dream about you, I can't ever touch or feel you. But last night, I could feel you. I could smell you. You have to be real, and you were reading my letters. I finally found a way to bring you back, and if it really are my letters bringing you back, I will keep writing them.

My days here at home still consist of fishing, boating, and just trying to relax by the fire at night. Ian, Sarah, and Justin came to visit me today, and we had a great time cooking out and catching up. I see Sarah every day right now as we are still filming in Philadelphia, but it was great to see Ian and Justin. They both are busy with new movies, but they are great friends who seem to never let me down. I wanted so badly to tell them about seeing you, but I can't. They'll never understand and will just worry about me, and they have done enough worrying about me to last a lifetime.

Seeing you last night has given me hope that you are still here with me, watching over me, guiding me, comforting me. You told me last night you are proud of me. I need to find a way to make myself proud. I know I need to be stronger. I am working on it. When you were alive, I felt like the strongest man in the world, and all of that strength got sucked right out of me when you died. But now, knowing you are here with me, I can sense a little of that strength starting to come back inside of me. I promise, Lark, if you just stay with me, I will do everything I can to keep making you proud.

Still yours,

Ryan

Lux Johnston turned off her thoughts and tucked away her fears of the water, and decided she would try again some other day. She would find her way back to the water somehow, but she wasn't ready yet. The waves crested just above her ankles, and that was the furthest she had allowed herself to go in a long while. The feel of the water against her feet brought back so many special memories of her childhood, but it also brought back the memory of that one fateful day, the one day she didn't want to remember.

Lux settled back onto her back deck and listened to the seagulls hovering over the water, looking for their next meal. She held onto her cup of tea while the smells of her surroundings intoxicated her. They were new smells to her; very different than the smells her hometown offered. Although she loved where she grew up, the smell of the lake that surrounded her home unfortunately came to signal danger and despair. It was a smell she no longer wanted to breathe in. The smell of the Jersey Shore symbolized hope and rebirth, and it was definitely a smell she could get used to.

The one familiar thing Lux had here was her father's best friend, Harry Wakefield. He had moved away to Longport with his wife when Lux was just seven years old. He has since divorced, but he stayed in Longport to run his flower business. Even though he had moved away, he kept in touch with Lux's father, and he and his family would come visit every fall. She loved Harry like an uncle, and she knew he would be there for her when she called and asked if he could help her find a place to live in Longport. And, of course, he did.

Seeing Harry was the one thing Lux looked forward to every Sunday night when he would come over for dinner. The two nights he had come over, he brought her a fresh bouquet of flowers and some of the best food she had tasted. She had offered to make him dinner the past two Sundays, but he wouldn't have it, and tonight was no different. "You need to experience the Jersey Shore cuisine!" he would say to her. She was very appreciative to have him in a town where she was a stranger to everyone.

Lux and Harry enjoyed the early evening bay breeze as they sat on her deck, feasting on a steamed lobster tail and a medium-well prime rib he brought from a popular steak and fish restaurant in Somers Point. While they conversed about her childhood and memories of his family's visits, she couldn't help but notice her neighbor dock his boat and clean it off. He had been rude to her when she tried to introduce herself, but she still couldn't seem to take her eyes off him. She felt drawn to him, even though she didn't want anything to do with him.

"That's Ryan. Have you met him yet?" Harry must have noticed her staring at him.

"Actually, yes. Last weekend." Lux responded. "But he wasn't very neighborly, I have to say."

"Really?" Lux could sense the surprise in Harry's voice as if it wasn't possible he could have been rude to her.

"Yes, really. He wasn't very nice to me."

"Well, actually, Ryan is a very nice guy. He's been through quite a lot the past year. You must have gotten him on a bad day."

Lux was intrigued. "What happened to him?"

"His wife died about eight months ago. He was devastated. They were very much in love."

Lux suddenly felt terrible, but at the same time, she felt relieved. Terrible that she was quick to judge him, but relieved that maybe he really was a nice guy and she wasn't living next to a jerk. "How did she die?"

"Cancer. They were only married for about six months, but they spent a lifetime together. He would come to the shop every morning that they were in town and buy her flowers. He never missed a day."

"I see him every Saturday night sitting alone, fishing by the bonfire," Lux said. "Last night, I saw him sitting on the dune."

"He and Larkin would sit on that dune together, feeding the seagulls and talking. The dunes were their special place," Harry explained.

It was starting to make sense to Lux. No wonder he was so protective of the dunes. They were special to him, and she could understand why he didn't want anyone on them. She was sorry he thought she was the one trespassing on them. She needed to find a way to prove to him that it wasn't her so she could have a chance at being his friend.

CHAPTER 4

The warm morning sun settled over the Jersey Shore as boaters and jet skiers awakened the bay from its slumber. Seagulls circled overhead searching for breakfast, and tourists left footprints in the sand as they began their day with a sunrise walk on the beach. It was the typical Saturday morning Ryan had grown to love. No matter how heavy his heart was right now, there was nothing like waking up to a summer morning in Longport. It had been three weeks since he had started seeing Larkin on the dune. Every Saturday night, she was there waiting for him, reading his latest letter. He looked forward to seeing her, and his visits with her were the only thing he could seem to focus on. It was affecting his work. His mind wasn't entirely focused on the movie, and during the week on the set, all he cared about was getting back to Longport to see Larkin.

Ryan sipped his morning coffee as he looked out onto the bay from his deck. He was looking forward to a boat ride on "Blue Eyes" later today. The boat rides seemed to be the only thing that could ease his mind. Just him and the surrounding bay underneath the endless sky where he would sit and write to Larkin as he waited for the flounder to bite the Peanut Bunker that had been casted out for their potentially unfortunate demise. But before he could spend his day out on the water today, there was something else he needed to do, something he hadn't done in a long time, and he wasn't sure how he was going to do it.

Ryan finished his coffee, locked up the house, and started his walk to the one place he hadn't been since the day Larkin died. It was the place where his life changed forever on that ill-fated day and the place where he almost lost his life. It was the day he couldn't keep his promise to Larkin.

The ringing of the bells as he opened the door to Harry's Flower Shop was so familiar, and he had opened that door so many times before. He had spent a lot of time here when Larkin was sick, but he had not been back since the day she died. It was the day he was hit by a car crossing the street, trying to get back to her as she waited for him to be there with her as she passed. But he never made it, and it has haunted him since. Sure, Larkin had helped him make peace with it. She had come back to help him see that he had in fact been with her that day, but it was still hard for him. And it probably always would be.

The familiar smell of roses and hydrangea welcomed back Ryan, and he quickly selected a bouquet of yellow roses that he would be giving to his mother later that day for her birthday. He wanted his visit to the shop to be quick, but as he turned to go to the line to pay, he realized that quick was not the way it was going to be. The line was unforgiving to Ryan's anxiety about being there. He reluctantly made his way to the end of the line, and as he waited, he noticed a familiar face perusing the flower cases. His new neighbor was having a hard time picking between a bouquet of daisies and a pot of blue violets. She was close enough that if he said something, she was sure to hear him. This was a perfect opportunity. He had actually wanted to run into her so he could apologize for the way he had treated her when she tried to introduce herself. He knew now that it wasn't her on the dune, and he felt terrible for accusing her.

"I would go with the blue violets," Ryan offered.

She turned to look at him and took a quick double take when she realized who he was. She had a look of surprise on her face, but she seemed to welcome his advice.

"Really? Why?" she asked.

"Because," he smiled, "violets are the state flower of New Jersey. A new flower to welcome you to a new state."

She smiled back at him, but he could tell she was trying hard not to. He didn't blame her. He didn't deserve a smile after the way he had talked to her before. She had a beautiful smile, he thought. He hadn't seen a smile that beautiful since Larkin's.

"Okay, I'll try the violets," she said, accepting his advice. "I have just the perfect place to put them. Thank you."

"Lux, right?" He couldn't forget a name that unique.

She nodded.

"I'm Ryan," he said as he offered his hand out to shake hers. She acknowledged his greeting and placed her hand into his. She had a strong handshake, but her eyes were timid and cold. She was hesitant to make eye contact with him, but when she did, she seemed distant and nervous. He wondered if she recognized who he was, but he definitely wasn't going to tell her unless she asked.

"I wanted to apologize for the way I treated you a couple weeks ago. I feel bad about that. I was having a bad day, and I took it out on you. I'm sorry. I know it wasn't you on my dune. I hope you can accept my apology."

She studied him for a moment before she offered him another smile. "Apology accepted."

He couldn't seem to take his eyes off her smile. "Well, welcome to Longport. If there is anything you need, let me know. I would like to make up for my bad behavior."

"Sure, I appreciate that." Her eyes were starting to warm up.

"Well, it was nice to meet you," Ryan said as he moved forward along with the line. Just as he turned away, he felt her hand brush his elbow.

"Actually, I do have one question. I'm new to the area, and I was wondering if you could give me some advice on things to do and places to see around here?"

Ryan hesitated for a moment, thinking about how he wanted to answer that question. His hesitation must have given her the wrong idea. "Actually, never mind," she recanted. "I don't want to bother you."

"I'll tell you what," he started to say as she turned to walk away. "The best way to see the barrier islands is by boat. How about I take you on a tour? It's the least I can do for my new neighbor I was so horrible to."

Ryan could tell that Lux wanted to accept his invitation, but she seemed uneasy and reluctant to say yes. "Umm, I would love to, but—"

"But," Ryan cut her off, "let me guess, you don't like boats?"

"Not really," she admitted.

"I'll drive slowly, and you can wear a life jacket. I promise nothing will happen to you. If you feel at all uncomfortable, I'll turn the boat around. Promise."

Lux still was hesitant to say yes, but the moment her eyes connected with his, she couldn't say no. "Okay, I'll give it a shot. I would love to see the islands."

"All right. Good. Meet me at my dock around two."

"Okay," she nodded. "I'll see you then."

The moment she walked away, Ryan suddenly wondered if he had made a mistake in inviting her out with him on the boat. He had wanted to befriend her, but now he was starting to think taking her on a boat ride was taking it too far. He started to immediately think of Larkin which made him feel guilty. He hadn't spent any time with another woman since her death, other than Sarah, and he wasn't sure if he even wanted to. Yes, Larkin was a ghost,and he understood that, but even so, he couldn't help but feel as if he was betraying her.

After having lunch with his mother, Ryan came home and quickly prepped the boat for his and Lux's ride that afternoon. He didn't know if it was the hot sun or his anxiety causing him to sweat more than usual. He was definitely looking forward to spending time on the water, but he couldn't decide if he was looking forward to spending time with Lux. She was still a stranger to him. Ever since Larkin died, he had a really hard time letting his friends and family inside of his head, let alone a stranger. But there was a positive to Lux being a stranger—she didn't know anything about Larkin. He was thankful for that because then he wouldn't have to talk about her. As much as he loved her, he didn't want to talk about her.

Lux caught Ryan's eye as she walked toward him on the dock carrying a small cooler. He started to feel more and more nervous the closer she got. Her presence had made it real to him. Even though she meant nothing to him, he was nervous to spend time with a woman for the first time since Larkin.

"Hi," she greeted him as she tucked a loose strand of her blonde hair behind her ear.

"Hey," he responded with a half-smile.

"I didn't know if I should bring anything, so I made us some sandwiches. I hope that's okay. I guess I should have asked. I don't even know if you like sandwiches—"

"It's okay," Ryan interrupted. He could tell she was nervous. "That sounds great. Thank you."

"Are you ready?" Ryan asked her as he took the cooler from her and placed it on the boat.

Lux studied the boat. "I think so," she reluctantly replied.

"Don't worry, you are safe. I promise." Ryan tried to reassure her.

Ryan took Lux's hand and led her onto the boat, careful to not let her lose her balance. He went to retrieve a life jacket for her from one of the compartments when he realized the one he was about to give her was Larkin's. She hardly wore it, only when they would go jet skiing, but it didn't matter. It was hers, and he had forgotten it was in there. He brought it up to his nose trying to see if he could capture her scent.

"Are you okay?" Lux interrupted his

memory. She must have noticed his reaction to the life jacket.

"Uh, yeah. Here," he said as he placed Larkin's life jacket back into the compartment and handed her his instead. "Wear this life jacket if you want. It should fit."

He tucked away Larkin's jacket before starting up the boat. He looked back to check on Lux, and he had to laugh to himself as he watched her clumsily struggle to put the jacket on. She caught him looking at her, and she couldn't help but laugh and throw her hands up in the air.

"I'm sorry, I can't figure this out," she said.

"No problem." Ryan approached Lux and knelt down before her, helping her to secure her jacket. He tried hard not to make eye contact with her as he quickly pulled the zipper up toward her chin, but as she quietly said thank you, her hand grabbed his elbow, and he couldn't help but connect his eyes to hers. She had green eyes that were as bright as emeralds, and her warm smile calmed his nerves.

"You're welcome," he paused as he reciprocated her smile. "Are you ready for your tour?"

Lux nodded yes, and Ryan slowly maneuvered "Blue Eyes" away from the dock. The sun's rays beamed off the top of the waves' crests as they splashed against the boat. The water was calm, and Ryan was thankful for that. He knew Lux was nervous, and rough waters would not have been ideal. As Ryan drove the boat out of the no wake zone, he sped up as he approached the back bays. It was a beautiful day, and the bay was packed with fishermen and jet skiers. He would periodically look back to check on Lux, and she would give him a smile to let him know she was okay. As he finally approached Sea Isle City, the first barrier island, he slowed the boat down so Lux could hear him talk.

"So, after Ocean City, Sea Isle City is the next barrier island. These islands are not as big as Ocean City, and there aren't as many year-round residents, but a lot of people come here to vacation." Lux studied the surroundings as Ryan proceeded slowly, taking her past the remaining islands of Avalon, Stone Harbor, and Wildwood.

"Wildwood is a really popular spot for vacationers, especially younger adults. Ocean City is what they call a dry island, meaning you will find no bars, but Wildwood isn't, so you'll see more college-aged kids here."

"And this is Cape May," Ryan explained as he stopped the boat at their last destination. "This is the southernmost point of New Jersey. There is a ferry you can take to Delaware from here. In fact, there it is," he said as he pointed out to the Delaware Bay. "You can see it." He turned to look at Lux, and she was hesitant to walk to him to see what he was pointing at.

"Here, give me your hand." He offered her his hand, helping her to the front of the boat. "Do you see it?"

"Yes." She nodded. The boat was gently rocking from side to side but just enough to challenge Lux's balance. She grabbed a hold of Ryan's arm as she started to fall, but Ryan grabbed her waist just in time.

"You okay?" he asked.

"Yes, thanks. I just have to get used to it, I guess."

"You will," he assured her. They locked eyes for a moment before Ryan realized it, and he was quick to look away. "So, are you hungry?" he asked, trying to turn their focus onto something else. "Do you want to eat those sandwiches you made?" he continued as he helped her back to her seat.

"Absolutely," she said.

"On the way back, there is a spot we can anchor at close to the beach and eat."

"Okay, sounds great."

Ryan again maneuvered the boat through the back bays to Corson's Inlet which nestled along the southernmost point of Ocean City. It separated Ocean City from Sea Isle City, and it was a hotspot for fishermen. He went there often, and he and Larkin would go swimming there from time to time. As Ryan anchored the boat, Lux prepared the sandwiches. "I don't know what you like, but I brought turkey and ham."

"I'll eat anything. Whatever you don't want, I'll eat."

Lux handed Ryan the ham sandwich as he sat down next to her. He noticed how organized and prepared she was. She had a blanket spread out on the floor of the boat with napkins and plastic utensils, mayonnaise and mustard, a bag of potato chips, and two bottles of water.

Lux broke the awkward silence as Ryan took a bite out of his sandwich. "Thank you for taking me out here. I really am having a good time."

"You're welcome. My pleasure. I come out here every Saturday anyway, so it's not a big deal. It's nice to have someone to talk to, actually."

Ryan stood up and grabbed a fishing rod. "Do you like to fish?"

"I never have fished, so I don't know," she replied.

"Well, do you mind if I set up a rod while we finish eating?"

"Of course, I don't. You love to fish, don't you?" Lux asked as Ryan baited the line.

"I do. I grew up fishing. It's a way of life for me."

"I see you fishing at night sometimes on the beach."

"Nighttime fishing has recently become a passion of mine. It helps me clear my mind," Ryan said as his line jerked with a bite.

"Got 'em!" Ryan yelled as he reeled his catch in.

"That fast? Do you always catch one that fast?"

"Not always," he said.

"Wow, that's impressive. I always thought of fishing as having a lot of luck. I guess that's why I never really tried it."

"Well, luck does have a lot to do with it," Ryan answered as he took a quick measurement of the catch. "But if you have the right bait and you know where to fish, you can usually come out on the good side of luck." Ryan gave Lux a quick wink as he threw the flounder in the live well. "That's a keeper."

"Do you always catch keepers?"

"No, actually, I catch more non-keepers than I do keepers. You must be my good luck charm today." Lux shyly flashed her warm smile.

Ryan took a glance at his watch. It didn't seem like it, but several hours had passed since they left. "It's getting late. Why don't we head back home?"

"Sure, okay."

It really wasn't that late, but Ryan wanted to get home to prepare for Larkin. Since Lux had been with him on the boat, he wasn't able to sit and write to her. He wanted to get home so he could write a letter. He had a lot he wanted to say.

Twenty minutes later, Ryan parked the boat next to his dock, tied the ropes to the cleats, and helped Lux climb out of the boat. He took the fish out of the live well and transferred it to his cooler.

"Are you going to eat that?" Lux asked.

"Yes. I am going to grill it for dinner."

"Listen, I don't want to interfere with whatever plans you may have, but I want to repay you for taking me out today. I am a really good cook, and I can make a mean flounder. Let me make you dinner," Lux offered. As Lux continued to talk, it was the first time Ryan really noticed her, and he was definitely attracted to her. He noticed the short yellow sundress she was wearing that was covering a cream-colored bikini top. It sat midway on her thighs, and it showed off her athletic legs and arms. Her blonde hair was pulled back into a ponytail, and her bangs dangled just above her eyes. He noticed that when she was nervous, she babbled on and on without taking a breath, and every time he made eye contact with her, she would look away. He definitely was making her nervous, but this didn't bother him for some reason. He actually found it endearing and sincere, and she seemed sweet, but it also made him wonder if she was nervous because she knew who he was. He wasn't sure because she didn't say anything to him about recognizing him, and he wasn't going to tell her unless she asked.

"It's okay if you don't want me to make you dinner...," Lux continued to babble on.

"It's okay," Ryan cut her off. "Sure, you can make me dinner. And then we'll call it even, okay?"

"Okay, great. I am just going to go take a

shower and gather some things together. Can I use your grill?"

"Of course," Ryan answered. "You go do what you need to do, and I am going to fillet the fish. Okay?"

"All right," Lux couldn't help but smile. "I'll see you in about an hour."

The smoke from the grill loomed into the twilight while Lux put the finishing touches on Ryan's earlier catch. It was a beautiful and clear August evening, and she was excited to have found a new friend in a strange town. Ryan seemed private, not sharing too much about his life yet. She had learned about Larkin from Harry, but she wasn't sure if she should ask him about her. Lux presented Ryan, who had been setting the patio table, with the grilled flounder topped with spinach and a mushroom sauce, and they sat down underneath the starry sky. Struggling to find a way to start a conversation, Lux was relieved when Ryan broke the awkward silence.

"This is really good, Lux. Thanks."

"Good. I am so glad you like it."

"You must cook a lot," he assumed.

"I do actually. I guess cooking to me is what fishing is to you."

They exchanged nervous smiles before Ryan took a sip of his wine to wash down his last bite. Lux didn't understand why she was so nervous to be around him. She was afraid he would think she was the most boring person to be around since she barely said a word to him the entire dinner. It wasn't like they were on a date, and she was the one who offered to cook dinner anyway. Even so, she had secretly hoped maybe it could be a date. She was definitely attracted to him, but she would still be happy to have him as a friend.

"So, what brings you to Longport?" Ryan asked, breaking the silence again.

"I needed a change of scenery. A new start," Lux began to explain. "And a friend of my family lives here, and he found me this place."

"Who's your friend?"

"Harry Wakefield. He actually grew up with my father, and we were close my entire childhood. He is like an uncle to me."

"Really? I know Harry. He's a good man." Lux wasn't surprised to hear Ryan say this. She knew that the two knew each other well from what Harry had told her.

"He's the best. We have dinner together every Sunday. He has really been there for me."

"Well, if you grew up with Harry, then you must be from New Hampshire. I know that is where he came from," Ryan said, giving Lux a half-smile.

"You're right. So, did you grow up here?" Lux asked, quickly trying to shift the focus off her. She didn't want to talk about her past. At least not now.

"I did. In Somers Point, which is right across the bay," Ryan said as he pointed across the bay toward the mainland.

"I'm familiar with Somers Point. I work in the hospital."

"Oh, you do? What type of work do you do?"

"I'm a general surgeon."

"Wow. That's impressive."

"Not really. It's no big deal," Lux said, trying not to come off as the big shot surgeon she was known to be in Boston. She really didn't think she was a big deal, but she was voted "Top General Surgeon in New England" the past two years. She would roll her eyes every time she would walk by her picture hanging in the lobby of her old hospital. She had no interest in the glamour her job had come to offer her. She just wanted to save lives.

As she was just about to ask Ryan what he did for a living, he stood up and walked to the edge of the deck, resting his forearms on the ledge.

"Lux, come here and look at this."

Curious, Lux eagerly walked toward Ryan and looked out into the bay where he was pointing.

"Do you see the dolphins?"

"Oh, wow, I do." Lux was excited to see the majestic mammals. She had never seen them up close before. "Do they always come this close?"

"Sometimes. Especially when the tide comes

in," Ryan explained.

"Wow. They're amazing!"

They made eye contact, and the smile he gave her had suddenly instilled the courage in her to ask him about Larkin.

"So," she paused for a moment. "So, Harry told me about your wife. I am really sorry to hear that."

"Thanks," Ryan said as he looked away from her and down toward the ground.

"I can't imagine how hard that must be."

"Listen," Ryan said, "thanks for dinner. It was really great, but there is somewhere I need to be. I'm sorry."

Lux was stunned by Ryan's sudden urgency to push her away. She knew it was because she had asked about Larkin, and she was suddenly sorry she had.

"Sure, okay," she said.

"I'll clean up everything. Don't worry. Thanks again," he said as he began gathering the dirty dishes off the table. He had reverted back to the Ryan she had met at the dock—cold and distant, not making eye contact as he dismissed her. She could tell he was angry by the way he slammed the dishes against each other as he cleared them off the table. She quickly scurried to the steps on the far side of the deck where it started to wrap around the house. She hated the way things had been left with

Ryan. They had a great day together, and she really felt they could be good friends. She decided she was going to try to make things better. She didn't know what she was going to say, and she didn't have much time to figure it out. As she turned back around the corner, she saw Ryan leaning against the railing at the far edge of the deck with his head in his hands. She could see he was hurting, and she suddenly felt guilty. Why did she have to ask him about Larkin? Why didn't she just leave it alone and wait until he started to open up about her? It didn't matter now. It was too late. The damage was done. She decided she would leave him alone. She had already ruined his night, and she knew there was probably nothing she could say to make it any better.

The moon had finally settled into the night sky, and Lux was still in awe of the view from her back deck. It definitely beat any view she had from her lakeside childhood house in New Hampshire, and it definitely was a far cry from the deep alleyways and high rise buildings that surrounded her Boston condo she lived in before she came here. The sounds of the seagulls twirling in the night sky serenaded her as she sipped her cup of wine. It was close to midnight, but she couldn't seem to take herself away from the beauty and the quietness she had begun to rely on for her peace of mind. She scanned the bay one last time to see if the dolphins that Ryan had showed her earlier were still swimming around. Just to her left, a small trail of smoke lifting into the night sky had caught her attention. She noticed it was coming from Ryan's bonfire on the beach, and she could see he had fallen asleep in his beach chair. She wanted so badly to walk over there and talk to him about what had happened earlier, but she figured he wouldn't want to talk to her, especially if she woke him up. She decided she would wait until next weekend when he got home. Maybe the week's time would allow his feelings to settle down, and he would be more willing to accept her apology. She had seen his kindness—the kindness Harry had told her about. She yearned to know more about him. She felt so drawn to him in just the short time she had spent with him, and she wanted to know why. Maybe if she opened up a little about herself and her past, then maybe he would begin to trust her and allow himself to open up to her. She just needed to find the strength to be able to do that.

The familiar scream of the faceless girl pulled Ryan out of his beachside slumber, and he quickly gathered himself and hurried inside the house. He was angry with himself that he fell asleep and angry with himself that he didn't write to Larkin. Now, he wouldn't get to see her. He felt foolish and guilty—guilty that he had spent the day with Lux instead of writing to Larkin. He looked at his watch, 1:00 a.m. Maybe she would still come.

Dear Larkin,

It's late. I'm late. I wanted so badly to write a letter to you again today so I could burn it for you, and then maybe you would come again, but I went out on the boat with the new neighbor, Lux, and before I knew it, time was lost, and now, so am I. I am so sorry, Larkin. Please know that the time I spent with Lux today was meaningless to me. She cannot replace you. No one can.

I found your life jacket today. I forgot it was still on the boat. The moment I touched it, memories of our time together on the water flashed before my eyes. I couldn't bring myself to give it to her to wear. Again, no one can replace you.

Maybe it's not too late. Maybe you will still come tonight. I will wait as long as I can.

Please come. I need to see you.

Ryan was thankful there was no wind tonight, but he decided it was too late to start a bonfire anyway. Instead, he just lit the corner of the letter on fire and threw it into the pit. He buried himself back into the beach chair and prayed she would come. He would wait all night if he had to.

As he waited, he found himself thinking about the day he had spent with Lux. He couldn't quite understand it, but he had felt drawn to her. He had felt a sense of peace in her presence—a peace that he hadn't felt since Larkin died. Sure, he was attracted to her, but that wasn't what it was. He had felt drawn to her in an emotional way, not a physical one, but she had had made him angry. Why did she have to ask about Larkin? Why? Why did she have to ruin the peace he had been finally been feeling?

An hour had passed and Ryan was starting to come to the realization that Larkin wasn't coming tonight. He hesitantly walked back inside and made the walk upstairs to his bedroom—the walk that had become so lonely the past eight months. He crawled into bed as sorrow and disappointment consumed his soul, but he was used to that feeling. He didn't know how to feel any other way. Ryan's eyelids slowly succumbed to the darkness of the night's calling. He was searching for a way out, but the only person who could lead him out of the darkness didn't come that night.

Ryan was startled out of his sleep by the blaring of the music coming from the stereo system. Even though it happened so often, he couldn't seem to get used to it. But tonight, it seemed louder than usual. He sleepily wandered downstairs to turn it off, and as he turned the corner from the bottom of the stairs into the living room, he saw Larkin standing on the back deck looking out into the bay. This was the first time he really took notice to how she looked. She was wearing an all-white lace dress, and her hair flowed down to the middle of her shoulder blades. She was angelic, beautiful, and most importantly, she was healthy.

Larkin greeted Ryan with a smile as he entered onto the deck to meet her. He mouthed the word *hi* to her, and as he got closer, she held out her hand.

"Dance with me?" she asked.

"Of course," he smiled, grabbing her hand and pulling her in close.

"You're beautiful," he whispered into her ear, and he pulled her in tight before spinning her around.

Larkin laughed as Ryan spun her playfully to the beat of the music. He loved seeing her like this. His last memories of her were of sickness, sleepless nights, weight loss, and pain. To see her like this now was a good start to helping him heal.

Ryan pulled her back in, chest to chest, and she rested her hand on the back of his neck. "You are so handsome." She smiled. He leaned his forehead in against hers, smiling through the tears as he told her he loved her.

"Thank you for the dance," she said, pulling away from his grasp.

"Larkin," he quickly pulled her back in. "I'm sorry I was late."

She grabbed his face and wiped his tears before placing her lips onto his. "I'm not," she whispered. She kissed his cheek and turned to walk away, holding his hand for as long as her arm would stretch. She climbed down the deck stairs and turned to look at him again. Her smile was as bright as the moon, and he watched as she turned back around toward the beach, trying desperately to keep her in sight for as long as he could. He was always afraid it would be the last time he would see her.

CHAPTER 5

There was an unusual chill in the late August morning air pushing through Ryan's half-opened bedroom window, and as he studied his face while he adjusted the knot in his necktie, he couldn't help but feel like he was back in time—back to the middle of January when he was adjusting the same necktie in preparation for Larkin's memorial service. In his mind, he replayed the conversation he had just two days ago on the phone with Lou. He had felt his heart skip a beat when he saw that it was Lou calling. He never called, so Ryan knew something was wrong. And he was right.

Ryan pulled up to the cemetery just as the service was about to begin. There were so many people in attendance to pay their tributes to a man who had served the community for the past two decades, a man who had meant so much to Ryan. He was the man who had helped Ryan fill so many of Larkin's days with beauty and love. As he sat among the hundreds of mourners, he closed his eyes, and once again, he played back that conversation with Lou.

"Ryan, it's Lou. I am sorry to bother you."

"You're not bothering me, Lou. Is everything okay? Is it the house?"

"No. Unfortunately, in this circumstance, I wish it were your house." Lou paused for a moment. "Ryan, I have some bad news," he continued. Ryan could hear the sadness in his voice. "It's Harry. He had a heart attack."

The rest of the conversation had become lost in a cloud of grief. All Ryan could remember was hearing Lou say Harry didn't make it. It had happened at the flower shop, and one of the customers had attempted CPR but to no avail.

Ryan was devastated. He held his head down throughout most of the service. He couldn't bring himself to look up at the coffin. He would occasionally scan the crowd, careful not to make eye contact with anyone. He was terrible in these types of situations. He always had been. Sadness was something he always had a hard time dealing with. It had been ever since his father had died. Dealing with sadness and grief made him feel like a fish out of water—unable to breathe. It was a feeling no one wants to have and a feeling he has had for the past eight months.

After the service, Ryan made his way to Harry's coffin, and he placed a single cyclamen on the top. It was perfect, he thought. Harry had given Ryan a cyclamen to give to Larkin on the day she died, and it symbolized good-bye. As he started to walk away from the coffin, he spotted Lux sitting by herself in the first row. He could tell she had been crying. He felt sorry to see her that way. He didn't end things too well with her last weekend, and he had still felt a little angry about her asking him to open up about Larkin, but he decided to put those feelings aside and offer her his condolences.

"Is this seat taken?" Ryan asked as he approached Lux.

"No," she softly answered, giving him a half-smile and a nod, letting him know it was okay for him to sit down.

Ryan sat down next to Lux and put his arm around the top of her chair, careful not to touch her shoulder. She looked at him, and all he could do was give her a smile—a smile to let her know that for just that moment, everything was okay between them. For just that moment, she could trust him and lean on his shoulder.

"I don't know what I am going to do. He was all I had here. I have no one now," she said, fighting back tears.

"Lux, I am so sorry for your loss. Harry was a great man. He meant a lot to this town. He meant a lot to me."

Ryan let Lux's head slowly fall onto his shoulder as she began to cry. "It's going to be okay," he reassured her, and he suddenly felt his arm fall down from the top of her chair to around her shoulders. They sat there for a moment in silence, and Ryan just let Lux cry. He couldn't help but feel uneasy about being there. He hadn't been to the cemetery since his father died several years ago, and as he looked around, flashbacks from that day consumed his mind. He suddenly knew he couldn't be there anymore, but he wasn't sure how he would be able to leave knowing Lux needed him.

"Lux, why don't you go home and get some rest? Staying here is not going to help." Ryan didn't want to be pushy, but he just couldn't stand to be at that place any longer.

Lux slowly lifted her head from Ryan's shoulder and nodded her head as she wiped her tears from her cheek.

"I'll walk you to your car," Ryan offered, placing his hand on the small of her back and guiding her down a hill toward the parking lot. They walked in silence to her car, but as soon as Ryan opened the car door for Lux, she collapsed into him, throwing her arms around his chest. Again, Ryan let her cry, holding onto her so she wouldn't fall.

"Are you okay?" he asked.

She finally gathered herself and released her embrace. "I think so. I'm sorry. I don't mean to be like this. I am just in shock."

"It's all right. I understand," he assured her.

Lux climbed into her car, and before she closed the door, she reached up and grabbed Ryan's hand. "Do you maybe want to go get some lunch? I really don't want to be alone, and you are really the only friend I have made here."

Ryan hesitated. He struggled to make eye contact with her.

"Look, Lux, I am sorry for what you are going through. I really am. I know how you feel. Believe me," he paused. "Believe me, I do. But I can't be what you need right now. I'm sorry." He *was* sorry. He didn't want to be so cold toward her, but he didn't know how else to act. He really was in no position to console her or be the shoulder she needed to cry on. He didn't know how to help her grieve. He didn't even know how to grieve himself. He had to figure out how to help himself first before he could help anyone else.

My Larkin,

Today my heart is heavier than usual. I was at the cemetery today. Harry died, but I am sure you already know that. I am sure you were probably there today welcoming him into heaven. Please tell him I miss him.

It took every ounce of strength I had to step foot onto that unwelcoming, cold, and lonely piece of earth. You know I haven't been there since my father passed. Not because I don't miss him. Not because I don't want to visit him. I just hate being there. I don't like the feeling of being surrounded by death, and that's how it makes me feel. I am glad you decided to have your ashes spread instead of being buried. It gives me peace knowing you are free amongst the clouds, the sun, the moon, and the stars. It gives me peace knowing your soul surrounds me and the air I breathe.

I went to see my father today. I almost didn't. I was sitting on the Triumph ready to drive away, but I just couldn't bring myself to leave. So, I took a walk. It took me a while to find his gravesite, but when I did, I sat down and just said…nothing. I just cried. I did manage to apologize to him for not coming to see him, but that's all I could say. You know I had a tough relationship with my father. He never really did support my decision to move away and become an actor, but if I have learned anything in the past two years, it's that you never *take anyone that means anything to you for granted. Never. It doesn't matter what they say, or not say to you; it doesn't matter how they treat you; it doesn't matter if they don't agree with the way you choose to live your life. All that matters is that they know you love them because now I know you take that love with you when you are gone. You have shown that to me these past couple of weeks. I didn't tell my father much that I loved him when he was alive. I was too busy focusing on me and focusing on his disapproval of my choices, and I never took the time to focus on bettering our relationship. I took him for granted, Lark. He is my one regret in this life.*

Before I left, I did manage to say one more thing to him…

I told him I loved him.

And I love you,
Ryan

The midnight moonlight shattered through the crest of the waves, and Ryan could see the tips of the dolphins' fins as they enjoyed a late night swim through the bay. Every Saturday, just before midnight, had been the usual time Ryan had come to expect a visit from Larkin. Tonight, he was yearning to see her more than ever. It had been a rough day with the funeral and going to see his father. He needed to see her calming blue eyes and feel her angelic touch. He had just finished burning today's letter, and he waited patiently. She wouldn't let him down. She never did.

A flock of seagulls were screaming in the distance, catching Ryan's attention as he was adding a piece of wood to the bonfire. He noticed they were enjoying a late night snack from another one of their old friends. He couldn't help but smile as she laughed while watching them scuffle over the last piece of bread she had thrown to them. Her happiness was childlike and pure, like she had never experienced one negative thing in her life. He knew that not to be true and could only hope that this happiness was everlasting. He was sure it would be.

He assumed heaven would do that to you.

She had come right on time, just like the past three Saturdays. He grabbed his bag of bread and walked down the shoreline to meet her.

"I see you brought our old friends something to eat," he said as he greeted her with open arms. She turned to look at him, and he was right. Her calming blue eyes were just what he needed. He couldn't help but just stare and smile at her as she walked into his open arms. She released their embrace and took his face into her hands.

"I am sorry about your day," she said, "but I am so proud of you and your strength."

"I get my strength from you," he responded.

"No, Ryan. You get your strength from you. You're much stronger than you think you are."

"I don't know, Lark," he said, taking her hand and leading her into a walk along where the water meets the sand. "I really don't know what I would do without you and your visits."

She was silent for a while. Ryan felt like he was troubling her, and he wondered if his incapability to move on was a burden to her. She paused their stroll and looked out into the horizon. "You were strong for Lux today," she said, turning back to him.

He paused. He was taken aback. She had never mentioned Lux before.

"I'm sorry, Larkin."

"Why are you sorry, Ryan? Don't be sorry. I want to know why you pushed her away."

"I'm not pushing her away."

"Yes, you are, Ryan. Why are you so angry with her? Were you really angry that night because she asked you about me, or was it really because of the way she made you feel?"

"Larkin," Ryan struggled to get his thoughts together. "She doesn't make me feel anything!"

Larkin took both of Ryan's hands into hers. "Can you do me a favor? In your next letter, write to me about Lux. Tell me about her. Tell me about how she makes you feel."

"Larkin—" Ryan was frustrated.

"Can you do that for me? Please?" She cut him off.

Ryan could feel the tide slowly rising against his ankles. His toes would slowly sink further and further into the sand with each rush of the waves, slowly sinking just like his heart. It hurt him to talk to Larkin about Lux. He couldn't understand why she was pressing him to open up to Lux. It felt like Larkin was pushing him away, but he knew if he wrote to her about what she asked, she would keep coming to see him.

"Okay, okay. I will do that for you," he answered reluctantly.

"You promise?" she asked, staring at him with those eyes and that smile that he missed so much.

"I promise." And he did. He *would* write to her about Lux just as she had asked. But he knew it was going to be a hard one to write.

Ryan pulled Larkin in close to him, whispering in her ear that he loved her. She reciprocated before slowly pulling away from his grasp. As she walked down the beach away from him, he couldn't help but feel he was losing her and knew these visits were going to stop someday. He needed to make sure he held onto her for as long as he could. Ryan started to turn around to walk back to his house, but the sound of her voice whipped his body back around.

"Oh, and Ryan…" She waited for him to fully turn around to face her. "You're no trouble to me at all."

And with that, she turned back around, and he watched her walk until she vanished into the wind.

CHAPTER 6

Dear Larkin,

I have been spending most of the morning trying to figure out what it is I am supposed to write about Lux. I know that deep down, this is your way of getting me to open up my heart and mind so I can let her in. Why do you want me to let her in? Why? I don't understand.

Lux is the first woman since you to see me for me and not who I am thought to be. She sees me as Ryan, her new neighbor, and not Ryan Boone, the famous movie actor. I have to admit, it was nice to be around someone who wanted to be around me because they were interested in getting to know me as a person while not having an agenda. Although, between you and me, she must be living under a rock or she never watches TV or reads magazines to not recognize me. I am not trying to be all high and mighty, but I can barely walk down the street without a tourist stopping me. At least the residents are used to me being here. I actually think they feel sorry for me when they see me posing for a picture and signing an autograph for someone. But you knew that it never bothered me. It comes with the territory.

I know, Lark, I know. I'm stalling.

You asked me to write about how she makes me feel. It's hard to do that because I don't even know how to feel anymore. I haven't felt anything since you've been gone, and honestly, I don't know if I even want to feel anything anymore. It's so much easier that way. Of course, it's an amazing feeling when you love someone so deep you can't live without them. But when it comes down to actually having to live without them, well, that feeling is so empty, so lonely, and so devastating you swear you will never allow yourself to go through it again. Sometimes I wonder if I will ever be able to allow myself to feel again. Even if I wanted to, I don't know if I could, Lark. My love for you was larger than life, and I'm still alive, so my love goes on.

As for how I feel about Lux. Well, Larkin, to answer your question, I feel nothing for her. I only feel empty, lonely, and devastated.

I love you,

Ryan

Ryan folded up the letter, placed it in a waterproof bag, and tucked it away in a compartment before starting up "Blue Eyes." The back bays were rough today, and it seemed to have affected the fish. This was the first day in a while Ryan hadn't caught a keeper. In fact, he barely caught any flounder, let alone what he liked to call "junk fish." Any other day, it would have bothered him. But not today. It had given him more time to write. He needed the extra time to figure out what to say about Lux. He still really didn't answer Larkin's question, but he didn't know how else to. He truly didn't feel anything for Lux.

The mild bay breeze carried a familiar scent along with it as it nipped at Ryan's nose. The mixture of salt water, bait, and fish was not a scent most people would find pleasurable, but to him, it was the scent of home. Every time he smelled it, it brought back so many memories of his childhood and the recent past—memories of his past with Larkin. He could stay out on the water all day. It was his happy place. The only place and time when he actually did feel something. And that something was peace.

Ryan weaved his way through the bay back to his dock. He tied the rope to the cleats, put all the fishing supplies back in their proper place before grabbing the letter, and placed it in his back pocket. As he was rinsing the salt off "Blue Eyes," he noticed Lux in the distance, standing at the edge of the beach looking out into the bay. He studied her as she would cautiously take a few steps further into the water before changing her mind and quickly running back out. Watching as she performed this unusual behavior three or four times, Ryan didn't know if he should be worried or not. If anything, he was certainly curious. He knew she was in a fragile state since losing Harry, so he thought it was probably a good idea to go check on her. He barely knew her, so he didn't know how mentally strong she was. Maybe she was someone who was mentally unstable and was thinking about taking her life. Or maybe she just wanted to go for a swim, and the water was too cold. He figured it was probably the latter, but he felt like he needed to make sure.

In the time it took Ryan to walk over to her, she performed the same bizarre behavior two more times. As he approached her, she was scurrying out of the water back onto the beach.

"You okay?" he asked with a mixture of concern and confusion in his voice.

She quickly looked over to him, and he couldn't tell if she was surprised or just embarrassed to see him there.

"Oh…," she said as she had trouble getting her thoughts together. "Yeah, I'm okay." She chuckled under her breath as shook her head side to side looking down. She was definitely embarrassed.

"Are you sure?" Ryan pressed as he bent forward toward her, trying to get her to look at him.

"Yeah, I'm sure." She looked at him for a moment before gazing back out toward the bay. "I'm just trying to conquer a fear."

"Ah, gotcha," Ryan responded. It was starting to make sense. "You have a fear of water. Well, can I give you some advice?"

She looked away from the water and back to Ryan, letting him know his advice was accepted.

"Well, I don't think the best way to face your fear of the water is by trying to swim in the *ocean*." He chuckled. "There are plenty of other places you can go. I think the Y up the street has a baby pool..."

"Ha ha ha," she said, cutting him off trying not to smile. "I know how to swim, wise guy. It's just..."

"Fear of the ocean?" he asked, trying to finish her sentence.

Lux hesitated. "Yeah, I guess."

"So, let me get this straight. You have a fear of the ocean and of boats, and you bought a house on the beach? Do you think that was a wise decision?" Ryan asked with a bit of sarcasm in his voice.

"Wow, you're just full of yourself, aren't you?" Lux responded, pushing Ryan's shoulder back as he laughed at her. "I bought it because..." She paused, looking around at her surroundings. "I bought it because it's beautiful here."

Ryan couldn't help but agree. "That it is."

"And because I was told I would have friendly neighbors." She smiled. "At least I got one out of the two."

Her last comment caught Ryan by surprise. He welcomed her with open arms. He was surprised by it, but he definitely welcomed it. "Ohhh, I see how it is. Now who's full of themselves?" Ryan asked, laughing.

Lux couldn't help but laugh, too, and Ryan felt happy to see her smile. He hadn't seen her smile since he took her on the boat ride, and he had forgotten how beautiful it was. He could still see the hurt in her eyes. They were empty and filled with sorrow. He suddenly felt sorry about how he pushed her away at the funeral. Even though she was joking about the friendly neighbor comment, he wanted to prove to her he could be a good friend. Ryan had always thought of himself as being a good person. He had to be if Larkin had loved him, and he wanted to prove to Larkin he was still that good guy.

"Listen," he started to say as they continued to stare out into the ocean. "I am sorry about the way I treated you at the funeral. You didn't deserve that. Let me make it up to you."

Lux turned and made eye contact with Ryan. She studied him for a moment before she reached out and touched his elbow. "Apology accepted," she responded, offering a forgiving smile.

Ryan smiled back before looking down to the sand. He didn't know why, but he was having a hard time keeping his eyes secured with hers. "I didn't catch anything out on the water today, so I was just going to order some takeout for dinner. Would you like to join me?"

It didn't take long for Lux to answer. "I

would love to. Thank you."

Ryan was finally able to make eye contact with her again. "I was going to order in about an hour so you can meet me on my deck if you want."

"Okay, that sounds great." Lux grabbed Ryan's elbow again, and he quickly pulled away from her grasp before turning to walk back to his house.

"I'll see you in a bit," he yelled as he turned back to look at her. She nodded in agreement, and as Ryan trudged through the sand, he couldn't tell if he was feeling excitement or guilt. Larkin immediately came to his mind again, and he started to wonder if she would come see him later if he didn't burn the letter. He would just have to make sure Lux was gone before midnight so he could prepare for Larkin's visit. There was no way he was going to jeopardize his time with Larkin.

Soaking up the sun's final fading rays, Ryan nursed the last half of his glass of wine while he waited for Lux to arrive for dinner. He felt nervous to see her. She really was the first woman he had spent considerable time with since Larkin. He didn't know where Lux stood with him. He didn't know if she truly just wanted to be friendly neighbors, or if she was hoping for more. The way she looked at him and the way she always reached out and grabbed his arm made him steer toward the latter. He wasn't ready for anything more than just friendship, and he needed to find a way of letting her know that without hurting her.

As Ryan took a sip of his wine, Lux caught his eye as she walked across the beach toward his deck. She was wearing a long peach-colored beach dress that fell to her ankles. The spaghetti straps brought out her sun-kissed toned shoulders, and her blonde hair was long enough to brush the top of her shoulder blades. She was barefoot, and her toenails had been caressed with a touch of peach to match her dress. As she climbed the four steps leading from the beach to Ryan's deck, he realized he was having a hard time taking his eyes off her. Even though he was not interested in anything more than friendship, he definitely thought she was the most beautiful girl he had seen since Larkin. All he could focus on was her smile as she approached him. Her dimples were the size of the Grand Canyon, and her smile could light up the night sky.

"I brought us some wine, but I see you already got started," she said as her eyes shifted focus to Ryan's wine glass.

"Allow me," Ryan offered while he stood up, grabbing the wine bottle and taking it inside. Minutes later, he came back out with a glass of wine for Lux followed by a tray with six different Chinese dishes.

"I hope you like Chinese food. I guess I should have asked you first."

"That's okay. I love Chinese food," Lux responded, digging right in without hesitating.

Ryan didn't know if he should be troubled or humored by the way Lux just dove right in without a care in the world. She looked like she hadn't eaten in days.

"Hungry?" Ryan asked.

Lux looked up from her plate, clumsily slurping up a noodle. She slowly took the chopsticks out of her mouth and quickly wiped her mouth with a napkin. "I am so sorry," she said, obviously embarrassed as she looked down placing her forehead in her hands. "Yes, I am," she chuckled. "I worked a twelve-hour overnight shift, came home, slept, and barely had anything to eat. I am so embarrassed. I don't usually act like this."

Ryan found her embarrassment endearing. He was actually happy she felt so comfortable around him. "It's no problem. Eat up. There's plenty here." Ryan flashed her a wink to let her know it was okay, and she didn't need to feel embarrassed. He could tell she still was because she proceeded to eat very slowly and barely made eye contact with him.

"Twelve hours? That's a long shift," Ryan said as he dug his chopsticks into the fried rice, trying to take Lux's mind away from her latest humiliation.

Lux finally looked at him. "Yeah, it is, but I only have to do it twice a week, so it's not too bad."

"Twice a week? Wow, what kind of job is that? Sign me up," he responded sarcastically. He knew Lux was a surgeon, so he understood she probably had a crazy schedule.

Lux laughed. "Well, I wish I only worked twice a week. I actually do surgeries two days a week, one day of follow-up appointments, and the two long days are covering the emergency department."

"What made you want to be a surgeon?" Ryan asked. Lux was the first doctor he had ever met, except for the doctors that took care of Larkin. She was the first doctor he ever befriended.

Lux hesitated, and her eyes wandered off into the warm horizon. "It was expected of me, I guess," she answered, shrugging her shoulders. "And I guess I was too tired to put up a fight."

Ryan could tell he was stirring up some negative memories in Lux's past, but he was intrigued and wanted to know her story. He couldn't help but want to ask more questions.

"Do you regret it?"

"Don't get me wrong," she assured him. "I love saving people's lives. Love it. There's nothing like it. But it's the days when you can't save a life that are the hardest, and no matter how hard you try, you just can't save everybody. When you have to go look their loved ones in the eyes and tell them you did everything you could, and they start to break down right in front of you, well, no good day could ever make up for the despair you feel on those bad days."

Ryan knew exactly what she meant. All the good days he had spent with Larkin combined could never make up for the grief he felt when she finally passed. Ryan decided he would stop pressing Lux about her career. It was obviously a stressful one for her.

"What brought you to Longport?" he asked, thinking maybe this would be a happier topic of conversation.

Lux stared at Ryan for a moment, and although she smiled, he could tell something was wrong. "So many questions," she answered.

Ryan was sort of taken aback. Lux had pressed and pressed him to be her friend, and now that he was trying, she seemed unwilling to want to open up. Or maybe Lux was unwilling to open up because he had been so unwilling to open up to her. He didn't know if this was the case, but he suddenly realized maybe he should try to open up to her a little. It was only fair.

"I'm sorry," he apologized as they both went back to eating. "Look, why don't you share something about you, and then I'll share something about me. That's fair, right?"

Lux nodded in agreement as she twirled her chopsticks around in the carton of noodles. "Sure, that's fair. But, it's your turn now." She looked up at Ryan and winked.

Ryan laughed, shaking his head from side to side. "I guess you got me on that one. All right, what do you want to know?"

Lux studied him for a moment, and he could almost hear the questions swirling around on her mind. He was nervous about what she was going to ask. Would she ask about Larkin? Would it be about who he really was? He really didn't know how he would answer either of those questions.

"Hmmm…okay, do you think you will ever move from here?"

Ryan was baffled. "Really, that's what you want to know about me?" He couldn't believe she didn't ask him something more personal. He figured she was probably too scared after the way he treated her the last time she tried to.

"Nope," Ryan was quick to answer. "Never. I'm going to die in this house." And he did. It's where Larkin died, so it's where he wanted to die.

"What do you do for a living?" Lux continued with the questions.

Ryan studied Lux's face for a moment. Did she really not recognize him, or was she playing stupid? "That was two questions by the way."

Lux laughed. "Yeah, I guess it was. So, I owe you two now."

Ryan moved on to answering her question. "Do you really not know what I do for a living?"

"Forgive me, but should I know you?"

"Well, no, I figured maybe Harry told you what I did," he said, trying to play it off. He didn't want to come off as cocky.

"No, he didn't. I just know you're not around during the week. Are you a fisherman?"

Ryan chuckled. "No, not a fisherman, but I would love to be." Ryan gazed out into the quiet evening bay, daydreaming about what it would be like if he were a fisherman instead of an actor. He would trade it in to be out on the water every day.

"Well?" Lux asked, interrupting his reverie.

"How about I promise to answer that question another day. Right now, I am enjoying spending this time with you without having to talk about my job. Is that okay?"

"Sure, I guess so." He couldn't tell if Lux was confused or more concerned that he wouldn't tell her what he did for a living. "So, I guess it's your turn to ask me a question."

"All right, you ready?" Ryan asked, rubbing his hands together.

"I don't know," Lux answered, looking worried.

"Where in the *world* did you get your name from?"

Lux couldn't help but laugh. "Well, Lux means 'light' and I was actually born in a lighthouse."

"Really?" Ryan was intrigued.

"Yes, really. My mother wasn't due for another month, and she and my father were on a boat ride with friends when she went into labor. They were close to the Portsmouth Harbor Lighthouse in New Hampshire, so they docked, and while they waited for help, my father, who is a doctor, delivered me."

"Now there's a great story to tell your children," Ryan said.

Lux nodded in agreement. "Okay, so I guess I owe you another question."

"I'm still waiting for an answer to the first question," Ryan said, giving Lux a half-smile.

Again, Lux looked out into the distance and hesitated. After a moment, she finally answered as to what brought her to Longport.

"My brother was killed in an accident, and I needed to get away." Lux's eyes started to fill with tears. Her eyes never left the horizon.

Ryan immediately felt bad that the conversation had taken such a tragic turn. He watched as Lux carefully wiped the small tears that were starting to find their way down her slightly pinked cheeks. He reached out and grabbed her hand for just a few seconds to let her know he was sorry. He knew it must have been really hard for her to allow herself to be so vulnerable to a stranger, and he felt guilty about making her feel sad. Ryan decided the only way he could make it up to her was to allow himself to be vulnerable, too. He hesitated, trying to figure out exactly how he was going to get through this, but he decided he just needed to do it.

"You already know this, but…" He paused for a moment. "I lost my wife to cancer less than a year ago." He let out a deep sigh. He could tell Lux was appreciative of what he had just shared with her, and just like he had done, she reached out and grabbed his hand to let him know she was sorry.

Ryan and Lux spent the next few hours sipping wine and talking about their childhoods. Ryan talked about growing up fishing, and Lux shared her memories of her family vacations to the lake with Harry's family. She talked about medical school, and he talked about his brothers and how his father died. But for the rest of the evening, Lux never asked about Larkin, and Ryan never asked about her brother. It was an unspoken rule. They both knew the other would open up again when they were ready.

It was about 11:30 p.m. when Lux decided she needed to leave. Ryan didn't even realize the hours had escaped away from him so fast. He was actually sorry to see Lux go. He was having a good time talking with her. He hadn't talked like that to anyone since—well, since Larkin. Talking to Lux was so easy and peaceful, and it was the first time in a long time he didn't feel alone.

Ryan walked Lux to the deck stairs and held her hand to steady her as she carefully maneuvered each step. When she reached the sand, she turned and looked up to Ryan and thanked him for dinner and for finding it in his heart to be her friend.

"Sure, Lux. I guess you're two for two now," he responded, letting out a quiet laugh as he winked. Lux smiled as she shook her head, knowing Ryan was alluding to the smart remark she had made to him earlier in the day on the beach. They gave each other a quick wave good-bye before Lux walked away. Ryan watched her as she walked home. He was glad he decided to allow himself to open up to her. She seemed like a good girl, and he enjoyed her company. It felt good to have a new friendship that seemed so innocent and so real. Especially because Lux really didn't seem to know who Ryan really was. To her, he was just the guy next door. And that was the most important thing to him.

The bonfire was in full force as the dolphins were enjoying a moonlit bath, and Ryan was eagerly awaiting Larkin's arrival. As good a time as he had with Lux earlier in the night, he still wanted nothing more than to see Larkin's blue eyes. She was late tonight, and he was starting to worry she wasn't coming. His Invicta read 12:30 a.m., and she was never this late. The bay breeze was starting to pick up speed just like every minute that had passed since he last looked at his watch. His hopes of seeing Larkin tonight were diminishing, and the thought that he may never see her again consumed his mind. *Why wouldn't she come? She knows I need her. Why wouldn't she come?* As the time reached 1 a.m., the breeze was starting to become unsafe for the fire. Ryan hesitated, but he finally made the decision that he needed to put the fire out and go inside. He held out for as long as he could, but he had come to terms that Larkin was not coming.

Ryan tossed and turned, his mind consumed with thoughts of his time with Lux and with anguish that Larkin had not come to see him. He had no idea how he was going to get through the next week. The only thing he could think to do was to write her a letter. He would send it to her tomorrow before leaving for Philadelphia. She would most certainly come next week, he thought. She'd just have to.

My lullaby,

I needed you more than ever tonight, but you did not come. I would have done anything to hear your voice. As I sat waiting for you, I would close my eyes and remember the times you would read to me when I couldn't sleep. My dearest lullaby, I can't sleep. Where are you?

The other thing I couldn't stop thinking about was the question you had asked me the last time I saw you. I was hoping I could see you tonight so I could finally give you an answer, an answer that I never gave to you in my last letter. It's an answer I had promised to give to you. Maybe that's why you didn't come. I didn't make good on my promise, so why should you make good on yours.

I spent some time with Lux tonight. I followed your advice, and I allowed myself to open up. I have to say, it was the first time since you died that I have not felt alone. Maybe you were right, Larkin. Maybe I wasn't angry at Lux for asking me about you. Maybe I was angry at how she made me feel. I guess I finally have an answer to your question. I don't really know what I feel for Lux; I only know she makes me feel.

All my love,

Ryan

CHAPTER 7

Summer in Longport was slowly fading into the horizon. The nights were darker, winds were cooler, and the colors were starting to change. It was hurricane season, and today there was a warning for a tropical storm with the potential of becoming a category one or two hurricane by the time it hit the Mid-Atlantic coastline. As a result, Ryan wasn't able to take the boat out. All week while he was away in Philadelphia filming, Ryan was hanging off his last letter to Larkin. He was looking forward to coming home and hopefully seeing her again. He was having mixed emotions. He didn't know how to feel. He was high off the time he had spent with Lux last weekend, but he was also devastated that Larkin didn't come to see him. Being home today was the worst thing that could have happened to him. Instead of being out on the water where he felt at peace, he was stuck at home surrounded by memories of him and Larkin. He prayed she would come tonight.

Knowing he wouldn't be able to go out to burn the letter tonight, Ryan burned it late last night when he got home from the city. He spent the evening studying his lines before watching his friend Ian's latest film. He hadn't been able to get a chance to watch it until now. Halfway through the movie, Lux had called his cell phone. He was hesitant to answer. He was afraid that answering it could ruin any chance he may get to see Larkin tonight. But part of him was worried about why she was calling. He was worried that maybe she was having trouble with the storm, so he decided he would answer just to make sure she was okay.

"Hey, Lux," he answered. "Is everything okay?"

"Hi," she said softly. "Yes, everything seems to be okay. I was just wondering if maybe you wanted to wait this storm out by watching a movie."

Ryan hated to say no. It wasn't that he didn't want to, but he wanted to stay home in case Larkin came. He chose his words carefully to not hurt her feelings.

"I'm sorry, Lux. It's not that I don't want to. It's just that I got home really late last night, and I need to get up early tomorrow. I really need to get some sleep."

"Okay," Lux responded with regret in her voice. "I am sorry to bother you so late."

Ryan could sense the disappointment in her voice. He really wasn't trying to hurt her. "How about we catch a movie next weekend when I get home?" He hoped maybe that would help her see it wasn't that he didn't want to.

"I would love that," she answered.

"Okay. Sounds good. Listen, if you run into any trouble over there with the storm, please call me, okay?"

"I will. Thanks."

As Ryan hung up the phone, a subtle shadow caught the corner of his eye. He figured it was a patio chair cushion taking flight along with the hurricane winds. It was nothing new. He replaced those cushions every season. They were always among the storms' casualties as they blew through the Jersey Shore every summer. Ryan decided to head up to his bedroom for the night and light some candles in case he lost power. If Larkin came, she would know where to find him.

Ryan turned the corner at the top of the stairs into his bedroom, and just as he turned the light on, there she was, standing at the bedroom balcony door watching the rain pound against the window. Her presence was like a whisper—soft and quiet.

"I just knew you would come," Ryan offered to her as she stood with her back turned to him.

Larkin turned around to look at him, and her smile was all he needed.

"Hey," she said with a warm smile, and they stared at each other for a moment before he walked toward her. She placed her hand in his, and he led her to the bed.

"Will you lay with me?" he asked.

"Of course," she replied before curling up into his arms.

"You always know when I need you."

Ryan and Larkin laid tangled in each other's arms for a while, reminiscing about the many times they would lay together during the storms and how Larkin would read to him by candlelight.

"Hey, is there something you could do for me?" he asked her.

"Sure, what is it?"

"You never did finish reading your book to me. I was wondering if you could finish reading it to me now."

Larkin lifted her head up off his chest and smiled as she stroked his cheek with her hand. "Okay. I can do that."

Ryan reached over to the nightstand and pulled Larkin's novel *Jillian's Touch* out of the top drawer and handed it to her.

"Here's the finished product. I have been meaning to show it to you," he said as he handed Larkin the book.

Larkin studied the paperback, flipping the pages, stopping every now and then to take in the scent they had to offer. "I always loved the smell of a book."

"I know you did," Ryan said. "I remember you used to always say that the smell of a novel can set the tone of the story."

Larkin laughed as she brought the book up to her nose again. "The smell of this one tells me it is a love story," she said as she winked her left eye at Ryan.

"Oh really? The smell tells you that? I guess it couldn't possibly be the fact that you wrote it," Ryan quipped.

Larkin just laughed. Ryan loved when he could make Larkin laugh. Her laugh symbolized a time of happiness and healthiness, a time when nothing else mattered but each other.

"You left off at chapter eight. I marked it," Ryan said as Larkin sank back down into his arms. The back of her head rested under his chin and against his chest. His arms swallowed her as she opened up the book and began to read. Ryan only interrupted her once, after chapter ten, to tell her he loved her. He never thought he would ever get to hear his lullaby again. But she was here and he never felt more alive.

My Favorite Lullaby,

Waves crashing against the earth. Fireworks lighting up the night sky. A favorite song. A child's laughter. I hear all of these when I hear your voice. You read to me last night. I never thought I would ever be able to hear my lullaby again. I fell asleep to your magical voice, and I haven't slept like I did last night since you died. But it tears me apart that I couldn't stay awake. I didn't get a chance to say good-bye. When I woke up, I thought for just a moment that I had been dreaming until I saw the book laying on the pillow next to me.

I would give anything to have you read to me every night, but I know that will never happen. Even now, after you are gone, you and I continue to make memories, and last night was a perfect memory. Thank you, Larkin. Thank you for continuing to bless my life with memories. I look forward to the next one.

Love, Ryan

Dear Larkin,

I had dinner with your parents tonight. It is always so great to see them. I see so much of you in your father, especially those eyes. I love looking at all the pictures of you, especially when you were young. It brings back so many great memories. The house looks different since you died. Your mother bought all new furniture and fixtures shortly after. I think it was a way to keep her busy and her mind off losing you.

I haven't told them that I have been writing to you, or that I have been seeing you. I think if anyone would understand and not think I am going off of the deep end, it would be them. But I don't know, Lark. Something is holding me back from talking to them about it. I did tell them about Lux, though. They started to ask me questions about how I was holding up, and I didn't want to seem too off, so I mentioned her to them. It was mainly to make them think I have started to move on. I told them it wasn't anything serious, just a friendship, but they seemed genuinely happy.

Your mother asked me a lot of questions about her. Most of them I didn't know the answer to. She told me, "Well, you better start to spend more time with her so you can find these things out!" I was surprised. I figured she would be the one who wouldn't want me to spend time with another woman. She would think I was trying to replace you. You know how old-fashioned she can be. Once you're married, you're always married. There is no such thing as divorce. I never thought she would have forgiven me after Abigail and I got divorced, and I never thought she would approve of you and me getting married. But she eventually understood what we had, and I think that opened her mind a little.

We had a conversation that really helped me see things a little differently. When she was asking me about Lux, I got a little rattled and overwhelmed, so I excused myself and left the room to sit on the porch alone. Your mother eventually came out and sat down next to me. Let me replay it for you.

"I'm sorry. I didn't mean to leave in the middle of our conversation," I apologized. "Everything is a lie. I keep telling you that I am

okay, but I'm not."

She grabbed my hand as she rocked back and forth in the rocking chair. "I know you're not. You may be an award-winning actor, but you can't fool me," she said as she squeezed my hand. I couldn't help but chuckle. "I can see it in your eyes. That's how I knew you loved my daughter. It was in your eyes."

"I did love your daughter. I do *love your daughter," I was quick to respond.*

We sat in silence for a brief moment before she continued. "You know, Larkin came to us shortly before she died. She asked us to look out for you as if you were our own son. She asked us to help you move on and to allow yourself to love again."

"Of course, she did," I said, not surprised.

"Ryan. It's okay to love again. And I am not saying Lux is the girl you are going to fall in love with, but you are never going to find that out if you don't spend more time with her. And if you are lucky enough to love again, it doesn't mean you don't love Larkin. And nobody will ever question your love for her. Nobody. Not me, not Russell, and especially not Larkin. Do you understand me?"

"Yes," I answered, fighting back tears.

Your mother stood up and pulled me up out of my chair and wrapped her arms around me. "You are the best thing that ever happened to our daughter, and we are so thankful she got to experience your unconditional love before she died. Please, don't be scared that you are turning your back on that love by loving someone else."

She pulled away from our embrace and wiped away a tear from my cheek. "Okay?"

I nodded. "Okay."

I didn't have the strength to tell her the real reason why I am scared. Well, I guess a part of me is scared that I would be turning my back on our love. But the main reason is because I don't want you to stop coming to see me. And right now, seeing you is what I am living for. And I don't want to stop living.

Missing you,

Ryan

August was coming to an end. Ryan's weeks were filled with work, and his weekends were filled with visits from Larkin in between time spent with Lux. He had decided to take Larkin's parents' advice to get to know Lux a little better. They would spend Friday evenings having dinner and watching a movie together. As much as he yearned to see Larkin, he occasionally found himself thinking about Lux when he was away during the week. There was something about her that seemed familiar, but he couldn't quite put his finger on it. Part of her reminded him of Larkin. Not her looks or personality so much, but in the way she looked at him. Most people seemed to look through him and not at him, but Lux wasn't one of those people.

Ryan pulled his Triumph into the garage and headed inside to unpack his bag from the past week. He looked forward to a quiet Saturday evening on the beach with just him, a bonfire, and his fishing rod. He was anxious for Larkin's visit later tonight.

Ryan would have dozed off if it hadn't been for a sudden and heavy jerk of his fishing rod, pulling it right out of the sand. He quickly jumped out of his chair to pick up the rod, and he gave it a hard jerk to hook his catch. It was a lengthy battle, and the fish had been a formidable foe, but Ryan's experience as a fisherman had paid off. As he began to reel in his latest victory, a familiar voice echoed off the clear night sky.

"Wow, look at that!"

Ryan turned to look and saw Lux standing behind him.

"Hey, come here," he said to her.

Lux hesitated. "Hurry, Lux! Come here!" Ryan called out to her again.

As she walked toward him, Ryan raised his arms overhead, careful not to let go of the rod. "Come stand in front of me. Hurry!"

Lux positioned herself in front of Ryan, and he lowered his arms around her.

"Here, take the rod," he said as he carefully placed one of her hands on the rod and the other on the reel, careful not to take his hands off of hers.

"Oh gosh. I don't think I can do this!" Lux said, letting out a nervous but delighted scream.

"Yes, you can. I will help you. I promise."

For the next several minutes, Ryan and Lux reeled in the flounder together. He never let go of her hands, and as the fish finally surfaced, Ryan reached out in front of them and grabbed the line to pull it closer to them.

"Do you want to hold the line while I get the hook out?" Ryan asked, certain she would decline.

"Sure, okay," Lux replied without hesitation.

"Are you sure?"

Lux nodded, and Ryan handed her the line. "You have to hold it still, okay? It's going to give me a fight, so it might jerk the line a little. Just make sure you don't drop it."

Ryan grabbed the flounder and cautiously removed the hook. He studied the fish for a moment, shaking his head in pride. "Now that's what I call a doormat!"

"A doormat?" Lux asked.

"A doormat is a name for a large flounder, and this is probably the biggest one I have ever caught!"

"Really? The biggest?"

"Yeah, it definitely is. Just eyeballing it, I would say it is about twenty-four inches long. I average about twenty inches." Ryan took the fish and placed it in the cooler next to his beach chair.

"Well, congrats!" Lux said.

Ryan looked up at Lux as he was packing the fish down in ice. "I couldn't have done it without you," he said, and he couldn't help but smile at her.

"I am sure you could have, but thanks for letting me help. I have never fished before."

"You did great," Ryan said, locking his eyes onto hers. Their eyes remained settled on each other for a brief moment before a seagull circling the dune behind Lux caught his attention. He suddenly remembered it was Saturday night—the night Larkin always came. He wondered if she was already there feeding her old friend.

"Can you excuse me for a moment? I'm sorry," Ryan said, and he quickly walked over to the dune. His eyes scanned the sandbank as he walked around it. "Larkin? I'm here," he called out. He waited for a few seconds. "Lark?" Again, he waited, but she wasn't there. He hesitantly walked back over to the beach, looking back several times just to be sure she wasn't there. Lux had been waiting.

"Is everything okay?" Lux asked.

"Yeah. Sorry about that." Ryan knelt back down by the cooler and finished prepping the fish. "So, what brings you out here this late?"

"I was just taking a walk along the water and I saw you. I missed you last night."

"Yeah, I'm sorry about that. I didn't get

back into town until today."

"Can I ask you a question?" Lux asked as she sat down in the sand next to Ryan's chair.

"Sure," Ryan answered as he closed the cooler lid.

"What is it that you do for a living? You still haven't told me."

Ryan walked over and sat down next to Lux. He studied her face for a moment.

"Why are you looking at me like that?" she asked. Her expression was so innocent, so sincere.

Ryan sighed. "You really don't know who I am?"

Lux paused. "No." She chuckled. "Should I?"

"Well, no, not necessarily I guess. But most people do." Ryan looked away. "It's kind of nice you not knowing."

"You don't have to tell me if you really don't want to," Lux said, and Ryan could hear the disappointment in her voice.

"You watch movies, right?" he asked.

"Of course. I have seen a good bit of them."

"Well, then chances are you have seen me."

Ryan didn't say anything else, letting Lux study him for a while. Finally, he saw her eyes start to widen. "No way," Lux said, shaking her head. "Are you Ryan Boone?"

Ryan didn't say anything. He just nodded his head as he looked out into the bay.

"Okay, now I feel really stupid."

"Please don't feel stupid."

"I thought you looked familiar, but I never thought that you could be a celebrity living next door to me in Longport. I do. I feel really embarrassed."

"Please don't feel that way. It's actually really nice when people don't recognize me. That's why I like being in Longport. It's quiet. There's no media chasing me around. The neighbors know me, and people are used to me being here so they don't bother me. Most of the tourists don't come to this end of the island, so I don't run into too many people hounding me."

"Well, for what it's worth, I am glad I didn't know because I got a chance to know you as Ryan, my fisherman neighbor."

Ryan looked at Lux and smiled. He believed her. He could tell by the way she looked at him. "So, anyway, that's where I am all week. I am filming a movie in Philadelphia. I am also the lead producer so I have a lot more on my plate than just acting, so it keeps me pretty busy."

"Well, you can count on me to be the friend that you can escape to. I will always be here in Longport. And we can talk about anything you want other than being a movie star," Lux said, nudging Ryan in his arm. He laughed, and as they sat in silence for a moment, Ryan studied Lux as her eyes wandered off into the distance. He hadn't noticed before, but her beauty was overwhelming. She didn't even have to try. She had a way about her that made it hard for him to take his eyes off her. He couldn't quite figure it out. The more time he spent with her, the more he wanted to get to know her.

"You know, Lux, you can talk to me about anything too, okay?" Ryan said.

Lux looked at him with a half-smile. He could see her guard slowly coming back up.

"I'm serious, Lux. I'm here, okay?"

Lux reached out and grabbed his hand. "Okay," she said, nodding her head.

Ryan knew that Lux had been through some tough times with the death of her brother and now Harry. She never talked about any other family or friends so he didn't know if she had anyone to talk to. And she really hadn't talked to him much about it either. Not since the night when she first told him about her brother's death. He actually felt sorry for her. At least he had Sarah, Ian, and Justin to lean on when Larkin died. He couldn't imagine having to get through it all alone.

Screams from the seagulls hovering over the dune had caught Ryan's attention again, and he suddenly remembered again that Larkin was supposed to come. At least he had hoped she would come.

"Well, it's getting late," he said to Lux as he

stood up and began gathering all his things together. "Thanks for the visit."

"Sure. Anytime. I'll see you soon, right?" Lux asked as she dug her feet out of the sand and stood up.

"Of course. I need someone to help me eat this fish," he answered before giving Lux a wink and a smile.

"Okay. You know where to find me." Lux called out as she began the short walk down the beach to her home.

Ryan was careful to watch Lux as she walked away, making sure she got home safely. It wasn't a far walk at all, maybe about fifty yards, but he still wanted to be sure. After he put all of his things away, he grabbed some bread and walked over to the dune to pay a visit to his noisy friends. He climbed the sandy mound and waited as he threw the bread out to seagulls, quieting their hungry screams. The minutes turned into an hour and Ryan didn't want to admit it, but he knew Larkin wasn't coming. She would have been there by now.

"Well, it looks like it's just me and you guys tonight."

Ryan threw out the last of the bread, and as the birds flew away, he watched as their bodies turned into silhouettes as they crossed in front of the moon. The moon looked as if it was filled with gold, and its magnificent light bounced off the inlet's whitecaps, illuminating the entire beach. It was a sight to behold, and it was one he would have wanted to share with Larkin. He was devastated she hadn't come. The only thing that provided him any bit of comfort was that maybe she could see the moon from heaven, and hopefully she was looking up at that same moon, and their eyes were focused on the same thing at the same exact moment in time.

CHAPTER 8

The chirping of the crickets echoing off the sunset sky was serenading Ryan as he was putting the finishing touches on the dinner he made for Lux. The days were starting to get shorter across the Jersey Shore, and Ryan found himself cooking many sunset dinners. He had mixed feelings about spending time with Lux. He felt a mysterious connection to her, but he also felt that the closer he got to her, the further apart he would be from Larkin.

As Ryan waited for Lux, he sat down and read one of Larkin's letters. Every time he read one, he felt so close to her, and he needed to know that she was close by. Larkin too had been pushing him to open his heart, and he felt it would be easier if she was looking out for him. She seemed to always know what was best for him.

A knock on the door startled Ryan from the letter's tight grasp on his attention. It was a funny sounding rhythm. Three sets of two quick knocks, each set with a pause between them. He knew it wasn't Lou, and he wasn't expecting anyone except Lux, but she always comes to the back deck. Ryan placed the letter down on the kitchen island and curiously walked to the front door. He was surprised to see Lux standing on the other side.

"Hey, it's you," he greeted her with surprise and confusion in his voice.

"Hi, I was supposed to come over for dinner tonight, right?" She obviously was confused by his muddled demeanor.

"Oh yeah, I'm sorry. You just never come to the front door, that's all."

Ryan held the door open for her, and he couldn't take his eyes off her as she walked inside past him. She seemed to get more beautiful every time he saw her.

"Dinner isn't quite ready yet. Make yourself at home," said Ryan as he took the bottle of wine she had brought and guided her into the kitchen. "Let me pour you a glass."

Lux nodded as she sat on a stool at the kitchen island. As Ryan handed her the glass, her fingers grazed the top of his hand, and he couldn't help but lock his eyes onto hers and smile. She had a gentle and soothing touch, so much so that he didn't want her to pull away, and when she did, he reached out and grabbed her other hand, resting them against the top of the island.

"Did you have a good week?" he asked.

"I did," Lux nodded. "How about you?"

"It was good."

Ryan and Lux remained hand in hand as they traded smiles and talked about each other's week. Conversation with her was so easy, and the more time Ryan spent with her, the more comfortable he became. He didn't even realize he was still holding her hand until he paused the conversation to go check on their dinner.

"I need to go check on the dinner. I'll be right back," he said, squeezing her hand before letting go.

As Ryan stood over the grill, he caught himself smiling. He never thought he would hold another woman's hand other than Larkin's. He never thought he would even want to. But what was surprising him the most was not only that he was holding Lux's hand, but that he didn't want to let go of it. As much as he had tried to fight getting closer to her, every time he was with her, he found himself wanting to know more and more about her. His mind was slowly falling into her with each minute they spent together. He found himself thinking more about her, and less about Larkin, and he wasn't sure how to feel about that.

Ryan piled the steaks on a plate and headed back inside to prepare a plate for Lux. When he stepped inside the door and saw her sitting there, every feeling of excitement, happiness, and trust that he had started to finally feel had suddenly turned to anger and uncertainty.

"What do you think you're doing, Lux?"

Ryan abruptly asked as he quickly set the plate of steaks down on the counter and rushed toward her.

"Do you always go through people's stuff?" he continued, ripping the letter Larkin had written to him out of her hand.

"I'm sorry, Ryan." Lux stammered through her words, obviously caught off guard by his sudden coldness. "I wasn't going through your stuff—"

"Really?" Ryan interrupted her. "So, I didn't just see you reading this?"

"I just saw it laying there, and I was curious. I'm sorry. I'm really sorry, Ryan."

"This is personal, Lux. You shouldn't have read it."

"You're right. Again, I am sorry, Ryan."

Ryan turned and walked away from Lux. He folded the letter and put in his back pocket before opening the door to the deck. He turned back around and looked at Lux. He could see she was upset at what had just happened. Her eyes had started to glaze over with a thin layer of tears, but he couldn't find it in himself to feel sorry. He was angry that she had opened the letter and started to read it. He had trusted her with not pushing him to talk about Larkin until he was ready. But now she had broken that trust.

"You should go, Lux."

"Ryan, I really am sorry—"

"Please, you need to go," he cut her off again.

Lux hesitated for a moment. "Okay," she finally said. Ryan could tell that she wanted to say more, but she didn't. She turned and walked to the front door and let herself out. When he heard the door close shut, he let out a sigh of disappointment. He was so angry about what Lux had done. He never thought that she was that kind of person. He was more disappointed in himself. Disappointed that he had started to let his guard down. Disappointed that he had let her in to his world. But mostly, he was disappointed that the feelings he was starting to have for her were now gone. He had finally started to feel something other than loneliness, but now that feeling was slowly starting to fill into his soul again.

Dear Blue Eyes,

People say to always go with your gut, your instinct. Never overanalyze a situation. And my entire life, I have always done the opposite. There were so many times that I turned left when I should have turned right. When I have said things I shouldn't have just to get what I want. But in my line of work, you have to be like that. You have to find a way to stand out in order to be successful. Early in my career, I took movie roles that most other actors wouldn't have just so I could stand out (hey, I did win a Best Actor Award!). And sadly enough, I dated women that I normally wouldn't have just for the exposure. But in the end, those decisions ultimately led me to the one thing that I didn't overanalyze; the one thing that I went with my gut. And that was you. You were my right-hand turn. And you were the best decision I ever made.

These past two months, my instinct has been telling me to let Lux in. And like I always do, I wanted to turn left when I should turn right. I didn't want to follow that instinct. But then I remembered what happened the last time I went with my gut. You happened. So, I decided to follow it again and let her in. I found that I had made the right decision, or at least I thought I had. I was never more wrong, Larkin. How could I have been so wrong?

I was starting to feel like I was coming alive again. I was feeling things that I hadn't felt in a while. Not love, but the excitement that maybe it could become love. But now all I feel is disappointed and betrayed. Disappointed in her and disappointed in me. I should have turned left again this time. No more turning right. After all, the only right hand turn I made led me to you and you're no longer there. So there is no reason for me to go that direction ever again.

Missing you,

Ryan

It was a typical Saturday for Ryan. Fishing on the bay underneath a calm and blue sky. The whispering of the waves as they brushed against the side of the boat was the only sound keeping Ryan company while he packed up his gear to head back home. He was out on the water longer than usual today. The last thing he wanted to do was go home. He didn't want to run into Lux, and he was worried she would be out on her deck when he pulled up to the dock.

The sun was starting to settle behind the horizon and blue sky was slowly fading to black as night ascended onto Longport. Ryan pulled into the dock and quickly cleaned up before heading over to start a fire in the fire pit. He wanted to burn his letter as soon as he could. He was desperate to see Larkin. She didn't come last week, and he needed her more than ever. It was the perfect night for a fire. No breeze and the air temperature was just right. Not too hot and not too chilly. Ryan settled into his chair and waited. He decided he wasn't going to set up his fishing rod tonight. He didn't want to be distracted.

As Ryan sat waiting and hoping, he closed his eyes and thought about Lux and what had happened last night. He didn't understand how he could be so wrong about somebody. He had come to trust her, and he thought she would be the last person who would have betrayed that trust. She seemed so genuine and so real, and she understood what he had been going through. She was going through the same thing with the loss of her brother, and just recently, Harry. He would never push her to open up about them, and he thought she was doing the same with him. But he felt that her reading Larkin's letter was just that. She had overstepped her boundaries.

The serenade of the crackling flames was interrupted by two dolphins playing just beyond the waterline, and Ryan quickly opened his eyes to observe their playdate. Just beyond the flames, he saw someone walking toward him. He had a hard time making out who it was through the flames and the smoke, but as she came closer, he let out a sigh of relief.

"You came," he said.

Larkin kneeled down in front of Ryan and grabbed his hands. "You needed me," she replied. "My beautiful boy," she said as she stroked his cheek, "you look so tired."

Ryan turned his cheek into Larkin's hand. "I do need you. More than ever."

Larkin studied Ryan's face before she moved to his lap. She pressed her back against his chest and the back of her head rested on his shoulder. Ryan wrapped his arms around her, and he turned his head to kiss the side of her head. They sat in silence for a moment. Ryan loved when Larkin would just sit with him and not say a thing. She had always done that when he had a bad day. She always knew that he didn't need her to say anything. He just needed her to be there and that was enough. Just being in her presence had always made him feel better.

"Don't give up on her," Larkin said, finally breaking their silence.

Ryan turned his head toward hers. "Why are you saying that? You know what she did."

"She just wants to know you, Ryan."

"Larkin, she crossed the line when she read your letter," Ryan said, raising his voice.

"Well, you need to remove that line. Ryan, in order for you to allow yourself to love someone again, to allow someone to love you for that matter, you are going to need to open up about me."

"I understand that. I do. I am just not ready."

"Yes, you are."

Ryan shook his head. "No—"

"Ryan," Larkin cut him off, "yes, you are. Look at me." Larkin repositioned herself so their eyes could meet. "Look at me. You are ready, and you know that you are. You were finally starting to feel something for her, and you're looking for a reason to run."

"I'm not trying to run."

"You are. You're running from reality, and the reality is that I'm gone."

"Not really, Lark. You're here now." "I am here," she paused, "but I'm not really."

Larkin rested her forehead against Ryan's. "She needs you, Ryan. She needs you more than you need me."

"Why does she need me?"

"She just does, Ryan. She just does. You have to trust me." Larkin pressed her lips against his, and in an instant, she was gone.

The knock at the door startled Ryan as he focused on writing his latest letter. He knew who it was. He could tell by her signature knocking pattern. Three sets of two quick knocks, each set with a pause between them. He didn't want to open it. But he couldn't help but remember the last conversation he had with Larkin. *She needs you more than you need me*, she had said. He kept replaying that over and over in his head. Larkin had seen something in her, and he wanted to see what she saw. He just needed to find the strength to open his eyes. He sensed Larkin was there with him telling him to open the door. Again, three sets of two quick knocks. He placed the pen down next to the letter and hesitantly approached the door. Lux stood before him, holding a plate covered with tin foil.

"I come bearing gifts," she greeted him with an apologetic smile. "Maybe cookies can buy your forgiveness?" she desperately offered.

He hated how beautiful she was. He wanted nothing to do with her, but she had the face of an angel. Sure, she was nosy, but she seemed harmless. Maybe Larkin was right. Maybe she really did just want to know him. But he wasn't ready to love again. He didn't even know if he ever would be ready. But maybe he should try. Maybe it was time for him to finally let his guard down. "It depends. Are they any good?" He mustered a half-smile.

"Well, I am biased, but they did win best of Belknap County two years in a row."

Ryan pushed the door open wider to let Lux know he was okay with her coming in even though he wasn't really sure if he was. Lux walked inside and placed the plate of cookies on the kitchen island and sat down. Ryan could sense she was nervous by the hesitant smile she gave when she walked past him. He followed her into the kitchen and sat on a stool across from her. He could tell she was gathering her thoughts together so he decided not to say anything, and he just waited until she spoke.

"I'm sorry, Ryan," she offered, her voice almost as quiet as a whisper. He could see the sincerity in her eyes.

"I know you are."

"I wasn't trying to go through your things"

"I know," he interrupted. "The letter was laying out in the open."

"But still, I shouldn't have read it. I don't know what overcame me. I can't even begin to imagine what you must be feeling to lose the love of your life. I guess I just want to. I want to know what you're thinking and feeling."

"Lux," Ryan hesitated for a moment, "I want to be able to open up to someone someday. I really do. And I want you to be that person. But every time I think I am ready, something inside me just shuts down. I'm trying. I really am."

Lux reached out and grabbed his hand. "I understand. I do. I want you to know that I will be waiting patiently for that day. You can count on me.

Okay?"

Ryan squeezed her hand. "Okay," he replied.

"Again, I'm really sorry."

"Apology accepted on one condition," he teased.

"What condition is that?"

"That these cookies are as good as you say they are," he said, winking at her as he pulled a cookie out from under the tin foil.

Lux laughed. "Well, that should be no problem."

Ryan took a bite. "Best of your county, huh? I can see that."

Lux smiled and squeezed Ryan's hand. "I have to go to work. Do you want to watch a movie later when I get home?"

"I can't. I am going to visit with my mother. How about I do you one better? Do you want to go for a boat ride tomorrow?"

"I would love that," she said.

"Good. I'll see you tomorrow."

Lux smiled before she got up to leave. Ryan was happy that he had answered the door and let her in. He watched her as she walked away and out the front door. Even though he had been so angry with her, he still felt so drawn to her the moment she walked inside. He didn't want to get too excited.

She had let him down once, and he was worried she might do it again. He was anxious for tomorrow and curious to see if she could make him feel those same feelings he had been starting to feel prior to this disagreement. Ryan walked back over to the couch to finish writing the letter he had been writing before Lux came.

Dear Larkin,

I am trying so hard to understand what you have told me about Lux needing me. I can't possibly imagine someone needing me, or anybody for that matter, the way that I need you. But I am going to do my best to try and make sense of it. Like I always have, I am putting my faith and trust in you, and I am going to give her a second chance. After all, isn't life about second chances? You and I were given a second chance at love, and we turned out to be the greatest love of all. I can't imagine having a greater love than you. But if I can love someone half as much as I loved you, then I will consider myself the luckiest man alive.

Needing you,

Ryan

CHAPTER 9

The water's glassy surface was gleaming as Ryan motored "Blue Eyes" through the mazes of the back bays. It was the perfect day to take Lux out on the boat. There was no wind, and it was the perfect temperature. The sun was as bright as Lux's smile, and Ryan couldn't help but keep looking back at her. He was happy that he had decided to give her another chance.

As Ryan maneuvered the boat around the bay's fingers, he found himself thinking back to last night's dinner with his mother. She never pressed him to talk about Larkin, but he could see the concern in her eyes every time he looked at her. She raised him and knew him better than anyone so she knew to give him his space. Ryan loved his mother, and he wanted to show her that he could be strong, just like she was when his father passed. He trusted her more than he trusted anyone, and the older he became, the more he relied on that trust. It was funny, he thought. It's not until people are older and wiser when they start to realize just how much they need their parents. And by the time they do realize it, many times it's too late.

Ryan hadn't planned on telling his mother about Lux. But as dessert was being served, he found himself opening up to the person he trusted most.

"So, I met someone," he said right before taking a bite of chocolate cake.

"You did?" his mother asked. She was so surprised, she put her fork down so she could focus on him. He loved that about her. She had always been a great listener, and she always gave her undivided attention to any of her sons when she knew they needed to talk.

"I did. But, Mom, it's just a friendship right now. Nothing more." He didn't want her to think it was anything serious and make a big deal out of it.

"Ryan, that's really great. Who is she? Someone you work with?"

"No. She's my new neighbor. She's a doctor over at the hospital."

"Well, do you want it to be more?"

"Mom, I can't even think about it being more." Ryan paused for a moment. "Every time I want to open up, I just can't. I look at her and sometimes all I see is Larkin and I feel like..." Ryan couldn't find the right words to say.

"You feel like you are betraying her?" his mother guessed.

Ryan shook his head. "No, I don't feel like that. Betraying is not the right word. I don't know how to explain how I feel."

"You feel like you are replacing her?" she guessed again.

Ryan thought about it for a moment. "Yeah, maybe that's it."

"Well, you and I both know that Larkin would never feel like you are replacing her. She would want you to move on."

"I know."

"All I can tell you is to follow your heart. Your heart led you to Larkin. I know she is gone, but your heart is still beating. So you just need to follow it. Whether it is toward friendship or love, just follow it. You have to trust that it won't fail you."

Ryan knew his mother was right. He knew that if he couldn't trust his own heart, there was no way he would be able to begin to trust anyone else. He had to start with himself first. Ryan slowed the boat down and anchored at his favorite fishing spot. He set up two rods, one for him and one for Lux. He could tell she was reluctant, but he assured her he would take the lead.

As the afternoon slowly faded away into early evening, Ryan decided it was time to pack up and return home. He hadn't caught many fish, but he did manage to snag two keepers. The conversation with Lux had been comfortable and easy. He didn't want it to end. Being around Lux was the only time he didn't feel lonely. Being with her was different than being around his family or friends. He could sense their sorrow for him. But Lux was a fresh start for him, and he was starting to look forward to it more and more.

As Ryan started prepping the boat to leave, Lux continued to carry on more conversation.

"If you could stop acting and leave it all behind to become a fisherman, would you?" Lux asked.

"Absolutely. The thought is already in my mind," Ryan answered without hesitation.

"Why don't you then?"

Ryan paused for a moment. He knew that in order for him to answer this question, he would have to talk about Larkin. Then he remembered what his mother and Larkin's parents had told him.

"Well, the movie I am filming now is something I needed to do. I promised my wife that I would go back to my life and go back to work." Ryan struggled to get his thoughts together. "But it's not just about going back to work. It's about honoring her memory. She was a writer, and she left behind an unfinished screenplay that she was adapting from a novel she wrote. So, I finished it, and now I am bringing it to life."

"Wow, that's pretty amazing that you are able to do that," Lux said.

"But this is going to be my last one. I'm done after this."

"You really think so?"

"In the past two years, I have learned a lot about what is important in life. And there is so much more to it than fame and fortune. Don't get me wrong. I love making movies. But because I was so busy doing it, I missed out on a lot of important things in life. The most important being love. I didn't realize I loved Larkin until she got sick. If I would have been around more, I could have had more time loving her. I can't get that back. And I'm not going to let it happen again."

"I haven't known you for very long, and in just the little bit, you have told me about her, you seem like you were really in love. I would give anything to have a love like that, even if it were for a short time."

"You've never been in love?" Ryan asked her.

"There were a couple of times that I thought maybe, but it turned out to be nothing. Like you, I dedicated most of my time to my work and never really gave myself much time for anything else."

"Well," Ryan said, "it was the best thing I ever had, and I am glad that I had it, even if it was for a short time."

Ryan studied the horizon as memories of his time with Larkin consumed his mind. Talking to Lux about her was easier than he thought it would be. He glanced over to her and noticed her studying the water. Just like that day on the beach when he saw her walking in and out of the water, he could sense that she wanted to go swimming, but was afraid to. Ryan stood up and reached his hand out toward her.

"Come on. Do you want to go swimming with me?" he asked.

Lux looked up at him, and he could tell she was surprised by his sudden invitation. She looked back out into the water before looking back up to him.

"No, that's okay. I'm good," she answered.

"Come on, Lux. We'll go together. You can wear the life jacket, and I will hold onto you. I promise I won't let anything happen to you."

"I know you wouldn't, but I just don't want to. Not today."

Ryan could see Lux was fearful, but he thought if he could just convince her that he would protect her, maybe she would reconsider. He wanted to help her overcome her fear. He knelt down before her and grabbed her hands.

"Lux, let me teach you how to swim. I can tell you want to go. I promise you, I will keep you safe. Come on," he said as he pulled up on her hands, trying to guide her up out of the chair.

"No, Ryan!" Lux yelled as she ripped her hands out of his. "I know how to swim. I don't need you to teach me. I just don't want to go swimming.

Please leave me alone about it!"

Ryan was caught off guard by Lux's outburst and anger toward him. He didn't understand why she had become so angry, but he was sorry he had upset her.

"Okay. I'm sorry. I didn't mean to upset you." Ryan stood up and pulled up the anchor before starting the engine to return back home. Lux didn't say a word, and he looked back at her a couple of times during the ride. He saw her wipe the corner of her eyes with her fingertip, trying to stop the tears from trickling down her cheek. Ryan was thankful for the loudness of the engine to help drown out the awkward silence that would have been between them the entire ride home. He felt terrible that he had upset her, but he didn't know what to say to help her.

Ryan carefully parked the boat up against the dock and secured it to the cleats with the rope. Lux gathered her things together, and Ryan was surprised she accepted his hand to help her climb out of the boat. As she stepped onto the dock, Ryan squeezed her hand gently before letting go.

"I'm sorry again, Lux. I didn't mean to ruin the day," Ryan apologized again.

"You didn't. I'm fine, really. But I do have to go, okay?" she replied.

"Sure, no problem."

Ryan watched Lux as she walked away. He knew that there was something more wrong than she was letting on. But he didn't want to push her. He figured she would tell him if and when she was ready.

The remainder of the afternoon, Ryan cleaned up the boat, walked over to the deli to grab some dinner, spent an hour or two studying his lines, and prepared the beach for his Saturday night ritual. He ignited the bonfire and fueled it with the letter he had written to Larkin last night. The night sky was as cloudy as his mind. His mind was consumed with thoughts of Lux and Larkin and trying to make sense of everything that was happening. He desperately hoped Larkin would come tonight to help him make sense of it all.

The screams from the faceless girl mixed with the screams from the seagulls hovering over the dunes rocked Ryan out of his fireside sleep. He studied his surroundings while he waited for the tired bogginess to clear from his mind. The night was as black as coal; his only light came from what was left from the bonfire and the few stars that weren't hidden behind the clouds. More screams from the seagulls caught his attention and when he looked over at them, he could see Larkin sitting on the dune, visiting her favorite friends. He gathered himself and walked over to greet her.

"Hey, beautiful girl," he said with a sigh of relief that she had come. He climbed the dune and sat down next to her, immediately taking her into his arms.

"I am so glad you are here, Lark. I need you."

Ryan pulled away from their embrace and Larkin grabbed his hands.

"I need you to talk to me, Larkin. I know you are here to help me. So, please help me. Tell me why Lux needs me. Tell me what my dream means."

"You still have your dream?"

"Every night. The same exact dream." Ryan paused and stared into Larkin's eyes. "Do you know why? Do you know what it means?"

"Ryan?" Ryan heard a familiar voice call out from the beach, just at the bottom of the dune. He looked down and saw Lux standing there. He quickly looked back to where Larkin had been sitting but she was gone.

"Hey," he answered back, trying to hide the disappointment he was feeling that Larkin was no longer there.

"Can I come up?" Lux asked.

"Sure." He was happy to see Lux, but he was more disappointed that he was no longer with Larkin.

Lux climbed up the dune and sat down next to Ryan.

"Who were you just talking to?" she asked.

Ryan didn't know how long Lux had been standing there, and he needed to come up with something quick so that she didn't think he was crazy.

"Oh, no one. I was just going over my lines in preparation for next week."

Ryan was happy to see Lux, but he could tell she seemed sad. He was hoping that maybe she would talk about what happened earlier in the day, but he wasn't going to push her.

"I am glad that I ran into you. I was out for a late night walk and saw you sitting up here," Lux said.

"Couldn't sleep?" Ryan asked assumingly.

"Nope," Lux answered.

They sat in silence for a moment. Ryan didn't know what to say. He had mixed emotions. He was missing Larkin, but he had wanted to talk to Lux too. He just wasn't sure where her mind was, so he figured he would let her strike up a conversation about whatever she wanted to talk about. Ryan glanced over at Lux, and he could tell she was trying to get her thoughts together. She must have sensed him looking at her because she turned to look back at him before looking down toward her lap.

"I'm sorry, Ryan."

Ryan was surprised to hear her say that. "What are you sorry for?"

"I'm sorry for getting so upset and snapping at you. I didn't mean to. You didn't do anything wrong, and you didn't deserve that. You were just trying to be a good friend and have fun, and I ruined the boat ride."

"No, you didn't ruin the boat ride." Ryan tried to assure her.

"Well, I feel like I did, and I'm embarrassed by the way I acted. Please accept my apology."

"Okay, but only if you accept mine."

"Why are you apologizing?"

"For upsetting you. I obviously said something that triggered a memory or something and it upset you. Believe me, I know how that feels. And I'm sorry for making you feel that way."

Lux looked at Ryan and nodded her head, letting him know she accepted his apology. He could see the sadness in her eyes, and he really wanted to be there for her.

"Listen, Lux. I am here if you need someone to talk to. Okay?"

Lux looked away, and her eyes scanned the horizon. Even though she was sitting right next to him, her mind seemed a million miles away.

"I am a damn good swimmer," Lux finally said. "Damn good." Lux looked over to Ryan before turning her eyes back to the water. "When I was eighteen, I qualified for the Olympic swimming trials. I had never seen my father so proud of me. He pushed and pushed me throughout high school, and all I ever cared about was not disappointing him. My brother, David was his pride and joy. He was the high school football star with straight A's. I was always trying to outdo my brother so that my father would look at me the way he looked at

David. And the Olympic trials were my chance to do that." Lux paused for a moment.

"I missed it by one second—one measly second—which, by the way, is a lot in swimming. I had never seen my father so disappointed in me. I will never forget the look in his eyes when I walked over to him after my race. He could barely look at me. I think that is why I went to med school. To avoid disappointing him anymore. But don't get me wrong, I love being a doctor. And I'm damn good at that too. Sometimes I wonder where my life would have taken me if I would have made the Olympic team. One thing I know for sure is that my brother would still be alive." Lux paused as she fought back tears.

She gathered her thoughts and began again. "Every summer, I would take a week off and drive up to New Hampshire and visit my family. David and I would always take a day and go to the lake and swim and lay out on the beach and just catch up with each other's lives. Last summer, there was a bad storm one day, and we were planning on going to the lake the next day. My mother begged us not to go because the lake was known to have bad rip currents after it stormed. But we insisted that everything would be fine, and she wouldn't have to worry about us. David and I had a tradition of racing from the beach to the buoy in the middle of the lake, and I would always win. He always said he would beat me one day. Well, he wanted to race again, and of course, I always had to accept his challenge. Of course, I won again but when I looked back to see how far back he was, he was gone. I couldn't see him anywhere. I was frantically looking for him, screaming his name, but I couldn't find him. And then I heard him scream out for help, and he was on the other side of the lake. I raced to him, but I couldn't figure out how to swim against the current. I almost drowned trying to get to him, but I couldn't save him. I watched him drown. I watched him die." Lux started to sob.

Ryan reached his arm around Lux and let her rest her head on his shoulder as she cried. He didn't say a word. He just let her cry. After a moment, Lux continued.

"I don't think my parents have looked me in the eyes since."

"They couldn't possibly blame you, Lux," Ryan said. "It was an accident. They have to know that. You know that, right?"

"It doesn't matter. I was the older sister. I was always supposed to be looking out for him. I should have known better. That's all they see. They don't see me. They don't see how hurt I am. They don't see how sorry I am. That's why I left. I needed to start over with a new life in a new place with new people. When I am in the water, I am more at home than anywhere else. I am trying to, but I haven't been able to go back."

"Well, someone once told me time heals what reason cannot. I am just starting to learn that. Hopefully, you will too," Ryan said, remembering the words Larkin had written to him.

Lux continued to rest her head on Ryan's shoulder. "I think about him every day, and I wonder if he is okay. It's ironic. I deal with death all the time, and I never stopped to think about what happens after we die. Not once. Not until David died. All I think about is if he is okay. Do you believe in heaven?"

"I do," he answered without hesitation. He knew that was where Larkin was.

"Really? You didn't take long to answer that. What makes you believe?"

Ryan thought for a moment. "I don't know if I can explain it. Hopefully, one day, I will be able to."

"Well, I hope you are right, and I hope David is there."

"I'm sure he is."

Lux rested her head on Ryan's shoulder for a little bit longer before raising it to rest her chin on his shoulder so she could look at him.

"Thank you," she whispered.

"You're welcome," he whispered back, tucking a loose strand of her hair behind her ear.

Their eyes locked for a moment before Lux reached up slowly, cautiously placing her lips onto his. As the two had grown closer, Ryan had recently thought about how he would handle this moment if it were to happen. He never thought he would ever be ready to kiss another woman other than Larkin, and he couldn't fathom the thought of placing his lips onto someone else's other than hers. But as his lips met Lux's, he responded in a way he didn't expect. He accepted her kiss and reciprocated, caressing her cheek as their friendship took on a new level. As the kiss released, Lux opened her eyes, and she placed her hand on his face.

"Good night," she whispered.

"Good night," he replied.

CHAPTER 10

Dear Larkin,

I don't know how to feel right now. My heart is tired. Tired of missing you. Tired of feeling lonely. Tired of staying closed. I didn't think I would ever be able to open it again, but it felt good to do so last night. So, why do I feel so bad? I feel the closer I get to Lux, the further apart you and I become. I thought that I would never be able to get close to another woman. But when we kissed, I couldn't seem to take myself away from her. When our lips connected, I was completely hers at that moment in time. Just for that moment, I felt alive again. No grief or sorrow. For the first time in nine months, I felt again. But just for that moment. The moment we released our kiss, my thoughts immediately rushed back to you, and I suddenly felt alone again.

I still need to feel you. To see you. To talk to you. I need you to help make things clearer for me. I can't do this without you. I can't make sense of anything—my dream, my feelings for Lux, the times I see you. I am so afraid I am not going to see you again.

Every day I remember. Not a day goes by that I don't think about what you have told me about time healing what reason cannot. Time with you is what heals me. And I feel like I am running out of time. I need more time.

Please come back.

Ryan

Guilt and sorrow hovered over Ryan all day as he spent the day getting ready for the week in Philadelphia. Not only did he feel guilty about kissing Lux, he felt bad about feeling bad. As good as it made him feel, he still couldn't help but feel sorry it had happened. He didn't blame Lux for the kiss. He blamed himself for letting it happen. And he wasn't going to let it happen again.

Ryan wished he had had more time with Larkin last night. He felt his time with her was getting shorter and shorter, and he was worried that it would be coming to an end soon. He knew she wasn't really real, and he was okay with that. But he didn't want to go back to what was real. Real was Larkin's death. Her visits made him feel like she was alive again. They made him feel alive again. He didn't ever want that feeling to go away.

The crackling of the burning fireplace serenaded Ryan while he sat on the couch with a blanket and one of Larkin's letters to keep him company. He was missing her more than usual since her visit last night was cut short. His guilt wasn't helping matters much either. Reading her letters always made him feel closer to her. He swore that sometimes he could hear her voice reading him the words that she had written to him. The letter he was reading was the last one she had written to him. It was his favorite one. Her strength poured out in every word she had written. Even in her final days, she had somehow found the strength to write to him.

Halfway through reading the letter, Ryan got the urge to burn the letter he had just written to her. Something inside him had told him to burn it tonight instead of waiting till next weekend. Ryan went up to his bedroom to grab the letter out of the nightstand and brought it back down and placed it into the fireplace. He sat back down on the couch and watched the flames swallow it before turning his attention back onto Larkin's letter. Just as he finished reading the last word, he heard a familiar voice call out from behind him.

"That was the hardest letter I wrote to you," Larkin said as she walked out from behind the couch before sitting down next to him. "I had to say good-bye to you in that letter."

Ryan was relieved to see her. He thought her visits would stop after his kiss with Lux. He was afraid the kiss would have pushed her away, and she wouldn't think he needed her anymore.

"It's my favorite one," he said as he reached

out to grab her hand. "But not because you said good-bye, but because it shows how strong you are. I wish I could be as strong as you."

Larkin squeezed his hand. "All of the strength that I had came from you."

"Larkin," Ryan struggled to gather his thoughts, "Lark, I'm sorry about last night."

"Why are you sorry? There is no reason to be sorry." Her eyes were so forgiving.

"Well, then why do I feel so sorry? I know you are gone. I do. So, why do I feel like I am betraying you?"

"You have never betrayed me. Never. And you need to understand that moving on with your life isn't betraying me. Not moving on would be. And you would also be betraying yourself."

"I'm trying, Larkin, I am."

"I know you are," she said as she stroked his cheek.

Ryan grabbed Larkin's hand and guided her down next to him on the couch. He wrapped his arms around her as she rested her head on his chest.

"Would you do something for me?" she asked.

"Of course."

"Would you read to me?"

Ryan was surprised by her request. She was the one who always read to him. He had never read to her before. "Sure. What would you like me to read?"

"I want you to read the part of the screenplay that you finished for me."

"Okay, I would love to. I have to go upstairs to get it. You're going to be here when I get back, right?"

"I'll be here, I promise."

Ryan hurried upstairs to grab the screenplay. He was worried she wouldn't be there when he got back. But she was, just like she promised. He studied her beauty as she sat there waiting for him. For a moment, he pretended that she was real. That she hadn't got sick, and they were enjoying a quiet night together. That everything was just as it should be. He pretended that they just finished dinner and were going to enjoy a quiet evening in front of the fire, just talking and dancing to their favorite music. He would give anything for it to be real.

Larkin turned and saw him standing there, watching her. She smiled, and he couldn't help but smile back. He walked back to the couch and pulled her into his arms as they laid down together.

"You ready?" he asked.

"Yes. But before you start, I want to tell you something."

"Okay. What is it?"

"I left you something in the nightstand."

Ryan remembered the last time she had said

that to him. He could only hope that it meant the same thing again this time. Did she write him another letter? He could only hope.

"You did?"

"I did. But I want you to read to me first. Okay?"

"Okay," he whispered in her ear. He kissed the side of her head before he started to read.

Ryan spent the next half-hour or so reading the screenplay to Larkin. She never said a word, but just listened. He would pause occasionally and kiss her on the top of her head, and she would squeeze his arm to let him know she was still listening. When he finished, she turned to look at him and told him how proud she was of him for finishing it and writing it so beautifully. Ryan asked her to stay a little longer, and she promised she would stay until he fell asleep. He tried with everything he had to stay awake, but before he knew it, he woke up in the light of the morning sun, and she was no longer there.

Ryan made himself a pot of coffee and grabbed the morning newspaper from the front porch. He made himself comfortable on the couch and found himself remembering last night's visit with Larkin in between reading the fishing forecast and yesterday's sports scores. Seeing her had made him feel a little less guilty about the kiss with Lux. But he still wasn't going to let it happen again.

In the newspaper, Ryan found an article in the local section about an elderly woman receiving a twenty-year-old letter in the mail that had gotten lost. It suddenly triggered the memory of Larkin, telling him she left him something in the nightstand. How could he forget? He rushed upstairs to his bedroom and frantically searched through his nightstand. But there was no letter to be found. He didn't understand why she would tell him that she had left him something there if she hadn't. Ryan started to doubt himself and his visit with Larkin. Maybe he had been dreaming. Maybe her ghost wasn't real and every one of her visits had been a dream. But he refused to believe that. There was one way he could find out.

Ryan rushed back downstairs to the couch to check if the screenplay was there. And much to his relief, there it was sitting on the coffee table. Unless he had been sleepwalking last night, there would be no other reason that screenplay would be sitting there. He knew it was there because he brought it down to read to Larkin. He believed it.

Ryan went back upstairs to search the nightstand again. He flipped through all of Larkin's letters and other random papers he stored there, but there was nothing new or different that hadn't been in there before. He started to wonder if maybe she didn't leave a letter. Maybe it was something else. He decided to empty everything out of the drawer to see if anything else was stuck in there, but again, his search came up empty. He placed everything back into the nightstand, and when he tried to shut it closed, the drawer became stuck and wouldn't move. As Ryan lifted the drawer out of the slides, a sealed envelope that had been stuck between the back of the drawer and nightstand fell to the floor. Ryan placed the drawer down before kneeling down to grab the letter. His heart was pounding with the anticipation that Larkin had written him another letter.

The envelope was bent in the upper right hand corner from being stuck, and the top edge was slightly frayed from the friction of being slid in and out of the drawer for the past nine months. The envelope had fallen facedown, and Ryan took a deep breath before slowly turning it around to see what name had been written on the front. His excitement quickly turned to disappointment as he read what Larkin had penned on the front of the envelope. The words were starting to fade, but not enough to alter his ability to read them. Ryan rubbed his fingers across the words, knowing that Larkin's hands had once touched that same spot. He held the envelope for a moment before placing it down on the nightstand. His disappointment slowly started to fade, and instead, his heart began to feel relief. Not relief for his sake, but relief for the intended recipient of this letter. Relief that they would get to feel the same closeness that he feels when he reads her letters.

Ryan gathered all his things together for the next two weeks and even though he needed to be in Philadelphia in a couple of hours, there was one thing he needed to do. Ryan jumped on his Triumph and drove across the Longport Bridge into Somers Point, and although it was only a fifteen-minute drive, it felt like an eternity. His heart was heavy and anxious at the same time. He felt good about what he was about to do, but he was also nervous. Nervous that he was about to unsettle the peace that they had made with her death. They would never stop grieving, but they had made peace with it and had learned to deal with it. He was worried that was all about to come crashing down, but he needed to do it for Larkin.

Ryan parked his motorcycle along the street curb, and he placed his helmet under his arm. He reached up to the pocket inside of his leather jacket to make sure the letter was still there. He hesitantly walked up to the front door and rang the doorbell. They weren't expecting him, but he knew they would be happy to see him. They always were.

The front door opened, and Larkin's mother was quick to open the screen door to guide Ryan inside and give him a hug. Her hug was soothing, and his nervousness started to slowly fade.

"Ryan! What a nice surprise!" Larkin's mother said as he she released their embrace. "Please, come in," she said, guiding him into the living room where Larkin's father was sitting reading the newspaper.

Larkin's father stood up and reached out his hand toward Ryan. "How are you, son?" he greeted him.

Ryan accepted his father-in-law's handshake. "I am doing well, thank you. Please sit down," he said, before joining Larkin's mother who was sitting on the couch.

"I am surprised to see you here. Are you finished filming the movie?" Joan asked.

"No, not yet. But soon. Actually, I am on my way to Philadelphia now, but I wanted to stop here first. I have something to give to you two."

Ryan made eye contact with the both of them before looking down to gather his thoughts. He wished he had rehearsed this, but he didn't and now he was struggling for the right words.

"Is everything okay?" Larkin's father asked.

"Yeah, everything is okay." Ryan hesitated for a moment. "I was going through my nightstand this morning, and I found something that had been stuck in the back of it. I just wish I would have found it sooner, and I am really sorry for that."

"What is it?" asked Joan.

Ryan reached inside of his pocket and pulled out the letter with the faded letters that read "Mom and Dad" on the front. "It's a letter. To you…" Ryan paused, "from Larkin."

"Oh my gosh." Joan raised her hand up to her mouth as she let out a sigh of disbelief.

"I am so sorry that I didn't find it earlier."

"Ryan, no. Please don't be sorry," Joan said as she reached out to grab the letter from Ryan.

Ryan watched Larkin's mother as she caressed the envelope, much like he did when he first opened his letters. He looked over to Russell who gave him a half-smile and a nod of thanks.

"Well, I will leave you two to read it. I need to go," Ryan said as he stood up.

Joan stood up next to him and wrapped her arms around him. "Thank you so much, Ryan. We love you very much. This is the best gift you could have given us."

Ryan pulled away from Joan's hug and looked at her. "I love you too. Both of you. You two gave me the best gift of all. You gave me Larkin. Thank you for that."

Joan hugged Ryan again, and as he turned to leave, she called out to him.

"Ryan? Would you like to stay while we read the letter?"

Ryan was moved and surprised by Joan's offer, and he didn't know what to say. "That's okay. She wrote it to you two and you should be alone—"

Joan interrupted, "Ryan, we would love for you to stay and hear her words."

Ryan thought about it for a moment. "Okay, I would really like that."

Joan grabbed Ryan's hand and led him back to the couch. She handed the letter to Russell and asked him to read it. She sat back down on the couch and grabbed Ryan's hand.

RYAN'S LETTERS

Dear Mom and Dad,

If you are reading this letter, then you know that I have lost my battle. But know that it wasn't a battle in vain. Ironically, the battle to not die actually taught me how to live. Please know that I would have lost this battle so much earlier if it weren't for the foundation of strength, love, and perseverance that you two have built for me.

When you are fighting to live, you truly learn what is important in life. And you two are and always have been the most important things in my life. You raised me to be a strong and independent woman, and if it weren't for your love, I would have never been able to live as long as I did. The foundation of love that you brought me up on taught me how to love. Thank you for teaching me that. Watching you two experience life together so in love allowed me to see what love could and should be, and because of that, I was able to experience the greatest love of all.

Please continue to love each other and please transfer all of the love that you had for me onto Ryan. Please show him that it is okay to continue to love and push him to find another great love. He will need you more than you know. More than he knows. He is the most loyal soul, and he will not want to let go of his love for me. Please help him to understand that loving again will be honoring the love that we shared, and by setting it free, it will always be surrounding him.

Thank you for giving me the opportunity to experience life and all that it has to offer. Although it was short, it was amazing, and I wouldn't change one thing. I journeyed through life happy and free, and I am certain that I will journey through the afterlife in the same manner. I will be watching over you, laughing when you laugh, crying when you cry, and smiling when you smile.

My love for you lives on in Ryan, so please take care of him. And every time you look into his eyes, I will be there looking back at you.

Love always,

Larkin

CHAPTER 11

Ryan was happy to be home in Longport after a busy two weeks of filming in Philadelphia. They were slightly behind schedule so they were trying to catch up with everything, and the sixteen-hour days were starting to catch up with him. The sun's rays echoing off the waves were a welcome sight for him. Much better than the sun glaring off the high rise building windows baking in the hot city sun. The sound of the waves crashing against "Blue Eyes" was also a nice alternative to car horns honking as they sit in the city traffic. Two more weeks, he had. Two more weeks of filming, and then he was done for good. No more filming and no more traveling. He was just going to stay in Longport and enjoy the quiet life, close to his family and close to Larkin.

Longport and the surrounding ocean towns were starting to quiet down as the tourist season was starting to come to an end. But the bay was crowded today, mostly due to the summer residents and tourists trying to catch their last keeper of the season. It was too crowded for Ryan's taste so he decided to call it quits. He guided his boat back to his dock, and as he cleaned it off, he noticed Lux arranging the furniture on her back deck. He hadn't seen her since their kiss two weeks ago. He wasn't intentionally trying to avoid her. He just had been away so he hadn't had the opportunity to see her. Secretly, he was sort of glad he hadn't seen her. He didn't know what to say and what she was expecting from him. At the same time, he felt like she probably thought he was a jerk for not contacting her after the kiss.

Ryan knew that he needed to talk to Lux at some point. He had come to care about her, and he didn't want to treat her like he didn't care at all. Besides, he had promised Larkin's parents when he left them two weeks ago that he would give Lux a chance, even though he knew there was little chance that it would turn into anything. But he was willing to try.

As Ryan was walking up to his back deck, Lux had turned around and saw him. They waved to each other, and he decided he would walk over to talk to her.

"Hey, stranger," Lux greeted him. "Haven't seen you around."

"Yeah, I'm sorry. I was in Philadelphia for the past two weeks. I didn't make it home last weekend. We're behind schedule so we're playing catch-up."

"Well, it's nice to see you." Lux smiled as she tucked a loose strand of her blonde hair behind her ear. He forgot how beautiful she was. He couldn't help but smile back.

"Would you like to come over for dinner tonight?" Ryan asked. He actually surprised himself by asking her that. He didn't know where that came from, just like he didn't know where the kiss came from. It seemed lately as if every time he was around her, all sensibility went down the drain, and everything he did or said was an uncontrollable impulse.

"That would be great. I would love that," Lux answered.

"All right. Six o'clock okay?"

Lux nodded as she smiled.

"Okay. I'll see you then."

As Ryan walked back to his house, all he could think of was how he was going to let Lux down later tonight. He wanted to be upfront with her and let her know that he just wanted a friendship. He wasn't ready for more. Not yet. Maybe someday.

After Ryan cleaned up the house for tonight's dinner with Lux, he decided he would sit down and write Larkin another letter. He had been so busy at work the last two weeks, he hadn't had the time to sit down and write to her.

Dear Blue Eyes,

I haven't been able to get you out of my mind since finding the letter you left for your parents. I have to admit, I was a little disappointed that it wasn't another letter to me, but after listening to your father read the words you wrote to them, I couldn't have been happier that they were able to get one last piece of you to hold on to. You never cease to amaze me. Even in death, you are full of surprises.

Our last visit together was one of my favorites. I loved reading to you. It made me wish I would have done it more often. But I guess you reading to me was always your thing. But even still, it was special, and I would give anything to be able to read to you again.

I keep hearing the words you wrote to your parents. The ones about pushing me to find love again and that setting our love free will surround me in it. I do want to love again, Lark. I so badly want to feel again the way I felt when I was with you. But I can't imagine feeling that way about someone else. I promised your parents that I will keep my heart open. And I will. I am going to see Lux tonight. I will see how she makes me feel. I will open up a little bit more. But if I don't feel it, if it doesn't feel as special as what you and I had, then I don't want it. I would rather be lonely than not feel what I felt when I was with you.

I don't know if it will ever happen, but if it does, then I will take your word that setting our love free will surround me in it.

Love,

Ryan

Ryan sat on the back deck waiting for Lux to arrive. He watched as the blue sky transformed into a sea of red and purples while the sun slowly sank under the distant waves. He couldn't decide if he was feeling excitement or nervousness, but now it didn't matter. His decision was abruptly interrupted as he saw Lux coming across the beach toward his house. He watched her as she clumsily trudged through the deep white sand, bottle of wine in one hand, the other pulling up on her long summer dress so as to not get her feet caught in it while she carefully tried not to trip. Ryan laughed to himself a couple of times when Lux would lose her balance. But she never fell, and when she finally made it to the bottom of his steps, Ryan stood up and walked over to her, offering his hand to help her up the steps. She chuckled as she accepted his hand.

"Next time, I think I am just going to walk down the sidewalk to your front door."

"Well, where's the fun in that?" Ryan asked, sarcastically.

Lux handed Ryan the bottle of wine before gathering herself together. He directed her inside and poured her a glass of wine as she sat down at the table. He tried not to make eye contact with her, but her beauty was like a magnet, and he couldn't help but look at her and smile. She smiled back, and he could tell by her mannerisms that she was nervous. Ryan left her to grab the dinner out of the oven, and he caught her looking at him on a couple of occasions. All he could do was smile, and he finally was able to decide that the feeling consuming his heart was definitely excitement.

Ryan finished preparing their plates, and he brought them over to the table. He placed Lux's in front of her before sitting across from her.

"I hope you like pasta," Ryan said.

"Wow, Ryan, this looks amazing. Where did you learn to cook? Everything you have made me so far is fantastic."

Ryan paused before responding. He didn't want to talk about how Larkin taught him how to cook. "Thank you. It's nothing special, really. Just a couple of recipes I picked up along the way. Don't get too excited. I don't have many more," he said as he laughed.

"Well, either way, it's great. Thank you."

"You're welcome."

Ryan and Lux ate their dinner in silence with awkward smiles in between bites. Ryan felt bad that he wasn't saying anything, but he really didn't know where to start.

"I am sorry, Ryan," Lux said, finally breaking the awkward silence.

"Why are you apologizing?" Ryan was thrilled that Lux had started a conversation, but surprised that she was apologizing.

"For kissing you that night."

"Lux, you don't have to be sorry. If anyone should be apologizing, it should be me for not calling you."

"Why didn't you call?"

"I don't know. I didn't know what to say." Ryan still didn't know what to say. "Lux, I'm just having a hard time with everything. If only you could understand what is going on in my head."

"Try to help me understand," she pleaded. Look Ryan, I know you lost the love of your life. I can't even begin to understand that. I am not trying to be the love of your life. I'm just trying to be a part of it."

Ryan placed his fork down on his plate, and he looked down for a moment trying to gather his thoughts together. He looked up to Lux, but a picture of him and Larkin that sat on a shelf behind Lux caught his eye. All he could think of was Larkin and her parents and how he promised he would try to open his heart. His eyes shifted between Lux and the picture before becoming locked onto Lux. His eyes got lost in her green eyes and just for a moment, a slimmer of a moment, he thought he saw his future. It was blurry, but he was certain he saw something there. He found himself smiling at her, and he couldn't seem to take his eyes off her.

"I want to show you something. Wait here."

Lux nodded and Ryan left the table and walked upstairs and into his bedroom. He sat on the edge of his bed and stared at the nightstand. He hesitated several times before finally opening up the drawer. He pulled out the large manila envelope, and he brushed it with his lips before walking back downstairs to Lux. Ryan sat back down at the table, pausing for a moment before making eye contact with her. Her eyes were so kind and caring, and for just a moment, he felt brave. He slid the envelope over to Lux.

"These are the letters Larkin wrote to me."

Lux studied the envelope, and he could tell she was surprised and touched at the same time. "Ryan, you don't have to show these to me," she said.

"I know. I want to. I have never said this to anyone before, but obviously, these letters are a blessing. And I know this is probably hard to understand," Ryan paused, "but they are also a curse. They're a blessing because they are the reason why I get up every morning, just so I can read one and feel close to her. But they are a curse because they make me miss her more and more, and I can't seem to move forward. But I can't bear to get rid of them. They are my reason for breathing."

"Well, maybe you don't need to get rid of them. Maybe just put them away for a while," Lux suggested.

"I don't know. I think I would always go back to them."

"Could you give them to somebody you trust to hold on to them for you?"

"Maybe. Probably." Ryan wasn't sure if he liked that idea. He didn't like the idea that the letters wouldn't be near him.

Lux must have noticed his hesitation to her last suggestion. "Okay. How about maybe just getting rid of some of them."

"What do you mean?" Ryan was curious.

"Well, I imagine these letters make you feel all sorts of emotions. Do any of them make you feel angry?"

Ryan thought about it for a moment. "Actually, yes. One does. The very first one."

"You don't have to, but can you tell me why?"

Ryan studied Lux for a moment. He could tell that she was doing everything she could to help him, but she didn't want to push him. He was starting to feel more and more comfortable with talking to her about Larkin.

"It makes me angry because it is when she told me she was sick."

"How often do you read that one?"

"Never," Ryan was quick to answer.

"Well, then why not get rid of that one? Maybe it will help you get rid of some of your anger."

Ryan thought about what Lux had just suggested. At first, he thought it was a bad idea. He didn't want to destroy anything that Larkin had left him. But after thinking about for it a little, he actually didn't think it was too bad of an idea after all. She was right. The letter did make him feel angry. And he never read it. So, why not? He wouldn't miss it.

"Okay, Maybe I can do that." Ryan grabbed the envelope and reached inside for the first letter. He walked over to the living room with it and sat on the couch in front of the fireplace. As he sat there, he started to feel very alone. He didn't know if he would be able to go through with it. He felt that letting go of one of Larkin's letters was like letting go of a piece of her. He knew he needed to do it, but he didn't think he could. He looked back at Lux who was still sitting at the table.

"Would you come sit with me? I don't think I can do this alone?"

"Of course." Lux walked over to Ryan and sat next to him on the couch. She placed her hand on his knee. "I'm here for you. Whatever you need."

Ryan was hesitant to throw the letter into the fire, and he found himself pulling it back several times. Lux must have noticed too. "Why don't you read it again? One last time so you can feel the anger again. Maybe that will make it easier."

"That's a good idea." Ryan slowly opened the letter and read it one last time, and as he read the words "My dearest Ryan, I have leukemia," he could feel the anger building up inside his heart. Lux was right. It was getting easier to let go of this one. Ryan folded the letter back up and he leaned forward, slowly releasing the letter from his fingertips into the flames.

Ryan sat back into the couch, and he immediately grabbed Lux's hand and watched as the letter slowly melted into black ashes.

"That's all you need to do," Lux said. "Just get rid of the ones that make you feel angry or sad, and hold on to the ones that bring back the happy memories—the memories that make you feel lucky to have loved her."

"Thank you," he said with a half-smile, squeezing her hand. "Thank you for being patient."

"Now, why don't you read one that makes you feel happy?"

Ryan pondered Lux's suggestion for a minute before realizing that he didn't want to read another letter. "Actually, right now, sitting here with you is making me feel happy. So, that's what I want to keep doing." And he meant it.

Lux smiled at Ryan and rested her head on his shoulder. Ryan reached his arm around her shoulders, and they just sat there together watching the fire. This time, the silence wasn't awkward. It was perfect and peaceful. Lux was bringing peace back into his life, and he was thankful. He hadn't felt this peaceful and happy in a long while. Ryan slightly turned his head so that his chin rested on the top of Lux's head. He grabbed her hand that was resting on his leg and his other hand caressed her arm as he inhaled the scent of lavender and lilies that emanated from her hair.

"I can't make sense of what I feel for you," he said softly. "I have never felt this way before. It was different with Larkin. It was easy. We were the best of friends growing up. There were no awkward silences or nervous smiles. The conversation was easy and comfortable. Everything is different with you. I don't know what to make of it."

Lux turned her head and looked up at Ryan. "I think it's a good thing," she whispered.

Ryan looked into her eyes and smiled. "I think so too," he whispered back. Ryan moved his arm out from around her shoulders and turned to face her. He grabbed her face with both hands and again whispered, "I think so, too," before bringing her lips to his. It was a slow, romantic kiss, and Ryan felt himself release it so he could look into her eyes. He wanted to see if he could see his future again like he did earlier. She smiled at him, her eyes locking onto his. Her smile was so beautiful. He couldn't help but kiss her again. This time, the kiss was much longer and more passionate. It felt different than their first kiss just a couple of weeks ago. This time, it was more meaningful, and he didn't want to end it, but he knew he needed to—he needed to because he wanted to know how he felt after it ended. Would he feel guilty again? Would he want to kiss her again? Ryan slowly pulled his lips away from Lux's, and he studied her face before smiling.

"Would you lay with me for a while?" he asked.

Lux nodded before falling into Ryan's arms as he guided her down next to him on the couch. They laid together for a while before Ryan felt himself falling asleep. He opened his eyes to see if Lux had fallen asleep herself. But he quickly realized that she hadn't when he felt her fingers caressing his hand.

"I want to take you somewhere tomorrow," he whispered.

"Where?" she asked.

"Somewhere important."

"Okay," Lux whispered, and he suddenly felt her fingers stop moving. She had finally fallen asleep, and he was okay with that. It felt good to hold someone in his arms again, and it was the first time he didn't feel so alone when he fell asleep.

Dear Larkin,

I haven't seen you in two weeks and I miss you. But no matter how much I have missed you, I haven't felt as alone as I usually do. I spent most of this weekend with Lux, and I have to be honest with you. She makes me feel nervous, anxious, and excited. These are good feelings to have, right? She has brought some peace back into my life. But most importantly, she makes me feel safe.

I did something today that I didn't think I would ever be able to do. I took Lux to meet your parents. But I felt that I needed to. I am trying to do right by you and your parents. I promised you and them that I would try again. And so that's what I am going to do. But as I was sitting on your parents' couch earlier today watching them talk to Lux and accepting her with open arms, I realized that I wasn't doing it for them. I wasn't doing it for you. I was doing it for me. And it is the first time since you have died that I have done something for me.

I was nervous to introduce her to your parents, but they were amazing. They were so excited to meet her, and I don't think your mother let go off her hand once as they sat on the couch talking. I know that your mom wants me to be happy. And I haven't seen her smile like she did today since you were alive. Every time I go to visit them, I always imagine you sitting there with me. But today I didn't. I was happy and excited to have Lux there. And as I watched her interact with your parents, I felt like I was back home again.

Amidst all of this excitement that I feel, I am also feeling scared. Scared of what is to come of you and me. As much as I care about Lux, I need to keep seeing you. I need to know that you are going to still be here when I need you. I am scared because you haven't come to see me lately. I fear that you will not come again. Even though I am ready to open my heart to Lux, I am not ready to let you go. Please don't go.

All my love,

Ryan

CHAPTER 12

Signs of autumn were creeping into Longport as the days were falling shorter and the nights growing longer. Joyous screams from children playing on the beach and boardwalk were replaced with hungry screams from the seagulls desperately looking for any food dropped or left behind. Falling leaves took the place of falling droplets of water that sprayed from the sidewalk sprinklers on those hot summer days. *Jillian's Touch* had finally finished filming, and Ryan was happy to be home full time. He was anxious to spend more time with Lux, but he also was hoping that Larkin would come see him more often now that he was home more. He had continued to write to her, and she had come to see him the past two Saturday nights. He had been able to open up about Lux a little more, and Larkin continued to encourage him to spend more time with her. Ryan had spent the past two weekends with Lux, but he kept it more friendly than anything. He wanted to keep Lux close but also at a distance. He wanted to be with her, but he was afraid being with her would cause Larkin to go away, and he wasn't willing to let that happen.

Ryan had planned a night of dinner and dancing with Lux to celebrate the end of his filming. He was becoming more and more excited to see her, and the time that they had been spending together was everything that he needed. He didn't feel so alone anymore, and more importantly, he didn't feel like he was drowning.

Ryan heard Lux's quirky knock at the patio doors, and he rushed over to let her in. He greeted her with a quick peck on the cheek and a long hug. Her scent was so intoxicating he didn't want to let her go. He offered her a glass of wine and guided her into the living room.

"Are you up for some dancing tonight?" he asked her as they sat down on the couch.

"That sounds great! I would love to!"

As much as Ryan wanted to take her dancing, he was nervous about it. The last time he went dancing was with Larkin, and he was afraid he was going to have a hard time with it.

"Great, but first, dinner," he said as he stood up and walked into the kitchen. "I ordered us some Chinese. I hope that is okay."

"Of course!" he heard her shout from the living room.

Ryan prepared their plates, grabbed some chopsticks and the bottle of wine, and set the table up for their dinner. As he was setting the table, he glanced over to Lux, and he could see her reading something. His heart sank when he suddenly realized that he had left a letter he had started to write to Larkin on the coffee table. He slowly walked over to Lux, and as he sat down next to her and their eyes met.

"Ryan, I wasn't snooping. I promise. It was just sitting here."

"I know," he said slowly, "I believe you. I meant to put that away."

Ryan was speechless. He didn't know what to say to Lux. He wasn't sure what she could possibly be thinking now that she knew he was writing letters to his dead wife. He couldn't even make eye contact with her. He just looked down.

"So, now you know. Now you know that I am writing letters to Larkin. And every time I write one, she comes to see me. That time I thought it was you on my dune, well, it was her."

"Is that why I see you sitting on the dunes late at night sometimes? You're with her?" Lux asked.

Ryan paused for a moment. "You probably think I am crazy," he finally said.

Lux reached out and grabbed his hand. "Ryan, no. I don't think you are crazy. Why would I think that?"

"Oh, I don't know. Maybe because I write letters to my dead wife who comes to visit me. You don't think that is crazy?"

Lux squeezed his hand. "No, Ryan. I don't."

Ryan finally looked up at Lux. "Really, Lux? Because I do." Ryan started to break down. "Sometimes I think I am crazy. I don't if it's real or if I am just imagining it. I don't know what to think."

"It's okay, Ryan," Lux comforted him.

"Is it?" he asked. "Because it's holding me back."

"Holding you back from what?"

"You. It's holding me back from you. I think it is why I push you away sometimes. I am afraid if I stop writing to her or if I give myself to you, she will stop coming to see me. And I don't know if I am ready for that."

"Look at me." Lux reached out and grabbed Ryan's face. "Listen to me. You are not crazy. You are sad and hurt. You are grieving. But you are not crazy. Do you understand me?"

Ryan slightly nodded as Lux continued to hold his face.

"I would give anything to see my brother again. And if I did, I don't think I would want it to stop either. You will find a way. You will. I believe that. And you can count on me to help you if you let me."

Ryan studied Lux's face for a moment. "You are amazing, you know that? You are everything I need." And she was. At that moment in time, Ryan realized that she was everything he needed, everything he wanted, everything he desired. Ryan reached out and pulled Lux's face in to his and he pressed his lips against hers. But the kiss didn't feel like enough to him. He wanted to be closer to her. He needed to be closer to her. Her kiss was the only thing that was helping him to feel normal again. He stood her up from the couch, and she wrapped her legs around his waist as he picked her up and carried her upstairs. Ryan and Lux shared a passionate night together, and he had gotten lost in that passion. Lux was beautiful. Her beauty was overwhelming to him, and he couldn't seem to get enough. No matter how close their bodies were, he never felt like he could get close enough or deep enough. Her touch was healing, and he didn't want it to ever stop. And as they continued to make love through the night, he realized he was falling in love with her.

Ryan and Lux spent the next day and night together mostly in bed, watching movies and eating takeout in between making love. Ryan hadn't felt this happy in so long that he almost didn't know how to act. It was an unfamiliar feeling, but every time he looked into Lux's green eyes and she would smile at him, all uncertainty was lost, and he felt normal again.

Ryan quickly shot up from his deep sleep, and all he could remember was purple and red skies and a screaming faceless girl drowning in the bay being whisked away by Larkin. He looked over to the clock on the nightstand, 12:15 a.m. As he studied the clock, he noticed the picture of Larkin that was nestled just behind it. Larkin. Ryan suddenly realized that he hadn't thought about her once this weekend since the conversation he and Lux had about her the other night. He also realized that he never burned that last letter he had written. The one that Lux had found. He quickly looked over at Lux to make sure she was still sleeping. He quietly got out of bed and walked downstairs to start a fire. She usually came around midnight so he thought there could still be a chance she would come. He burned the letter and waited on the back deck until about 2:00 a.m. She never came.

Ryan went back upstairs, but he couldn't sleep. He decided to sit on the balcony and prayed that maybe she would still come. As Ryan waited, he felt angry and guilty. How could he forget about her like that? He knew this would happen. He knew if he moved on, she would stop coming. He wasn't sure if he was ready for that. But now he knew for certain. He wasn't. He was devastated that she hadn't come.

Ryan was startled out of his sleep by Lux who had brought him a cup of coffee. She sat in the chair next to him.

"What are you doing out here?" she asked.

Ryan struggled to clear the tired fogginess out of his head. He grabbed the cup of coffee from Lux, but didn't answer her question.

"Are you okay?" Lux pressed.

Ryan rubbed his eyes and glanced over at

her. He was still overwhelmed by her beauty.

She was as beautiful as the sunrise. But as beautiful as she was, his guilt and sorrow were more overwhelming.

He looked down for a while before finally answering her question. "I think you should go."

"What?" He could tell Lux was taken aback and surprised by his request. Of course, she was, he thought. After the weekend they had, that's probably the last thing she would have expected to hear from him.

"You should go," he reiterated, this time in a firmer voice. "I'm sorry, Lux. This weekend should have never happened. It was a mistake." It killed Ryan to say that to her. He couldn't even look her in the eyes. She did nothing wrong. She didn't deserve it.

"A mistake? How can you say that?"

Ryan turned his head to look at the dunes just off to the right of the balcony. Lux must have noticed.

"Oh, I get it. She was supposed to come see you last night, and she didn't come."

"Lux, you just need to go. Please. I don't want to hurt you."

"Hurt me?" Ryan could hear her voice starting to crack. "It's too late. You already did."

Ryan really wanted to grab Lux and pull her into his arms, but he couldn't. He knew if he did that, he would take her back to bed and make love to her again. And he couldn't do that. He wanted to see Larkin again.

"Ryan, I meant it when I said I don't think you are crazy. And I know you know that she's not real. But I am. I'm real. I told you that I could help you if you let me. But you won't let me. She's not real. I'm real. This past weekend was real, and I can give that to you every day if you would just let me."

Ryan didn't know what to say so he didn't say anything. He just continued to look out into the bay, trying not to let Lux's crying tear him apart. He finally heard Lux gathering her things, and he could hear her footsteps as she walked down the stairs. He could see her walk across the beach to her house, and he could see that she was crying. He felt terrible for the way he treated her after the weekend they had just spent together. But he didn't know how else to act. He had changed back to the cold and distant Ryan. The one he had started to become comfortable with the past nine months.

My dearest Larkin,

Sad. Lonely. Cold. That is what I saw when I looked into the mirror this morning as I was packing my bags for the week. But it is a face that I am used to looking at. I was starting to not recognize myself the past couple of weeks. My face had turned from cold and sad to warm and happy. But now, my old familiar face is back. And I think it will just have to suit me until we are reunited.

I don't know what I was thinking, Larkin. How could I possibly ever think that I could replace you? I did what you asked. I let her in. And by doing that, I lost you.

I let her go, Larkin. I can't sacrifice our love for a new one. I know that you keep telling me that I am ready, but I'm not. I am not ready to allow myself to be without you. I am not ready to let go of the love that we had. But most importantly, I am not ready to let you down. I am here for you. Please, I still need you.

All my love,

Ryan

Ryan folded the letter and placed it in the front pocket of his luggage bag for safekeeping until he reached his destination. He was going to be away a little longer than usual this time. He wasn't sure where he was going, but he needed to get away. As much as he wanted to be in Longport, he felt a need to be somewhere else right now. He had mixed emotions about it. Being away from Longport meant being away from Larkin, although he wasn't sure if he was going to see her again. But leaving also meant being away from Lux, and he really didn't want to see her. He wasn't ready to see her. Not because he had hurt her, but because he was hurting too. He had fallen for her and seeing her face would just hurt him even more.

Ryan took a walk around the house to make sure everything was secure. He quickly walked over to Lou's to let him know he was going to be gone for a couple of weeks and asked him to keep an eye out. Of course, Lou was happy to. Ryan went back into the house to grab the luggage bag out of his bedroom, and when he came back downstairs, a familiar smell beckoned him to the living room. His heart quivered. He knew that smell. Ryan turned the corner and there she was.

"You're here?" he said as she turned to face him. "I didn't even get a chance to send you my last letter."

"I already saw it. I was watching over your shoulder as you wrote it."

Ryan approached Larkin, and she took his hand and led him to the couch.

"Lark, tell me what to do," Ryan begged, "tell me how to let go of you. Tell me how I can move on without you. Because I can't find a way."

"Ryan, you have to know that I am always here, even if you can't see me. Always. I need you to understand that you take the love with you when you die. You really do. Don't you remember?"

Ryan shook his head. "Remember what?

"Remember that night on the beach. The night you spread my ashes."

"Of course, I remember."

"Well, then you remember that you were there with me. You, and Ian, and Justin, and Sarah. You are with me every day, Ryan. You and I are in a place that we can shine together forever."

Ryan felt Larkin squeeze his hands, and they sat in silence for a moment as they stared into each other's eyes. He could feel Larkin start to pull her hands away from his. And for the first time, Ryan let her. He didn't try to hold on this time. Larkin reached up and brushed his cheek with her fingers. "My beautiful boy. Time heals what reason cannot. And it's time."

Ryan grabbed Larkin's hand and brought it to his lips. She stood up and started to walk away. He was pretty sure that this was the last time he was going to see her, and he knew there was nothing he could say to keep her here. He watched as she moved away from him. He started to call out for her, but he stopped himself.

"Oh, and Ryan," Larkin turned back to him as she was walking away, "you're not letting me down by loving her. You're letting me down by *not* loving her."

The brisk autumn wind blew right through Ryan's black leather jacket as he maneuvered his Triumph across the Longport Bridge. Halfway across the bridge, Ryan pulled the bike over, took his helmet off, and focused his eyes across the bay onto Longport. He could see his house nestled behind the dunes. He reminisced about the times he had spent with Larkin in that house and on those dunes. He felt a tear roll down his cheek as he swore he could see the two of them dancing on the beach. Ryan felt like he was leaving Larkin by leaving town. But deep in his gut, he felt like he needed to get away. Larkin promised him that even though he couldn't see her, she was always there. And he needed to trust that. He didn't know where he would end up, but he knew there was one place he needed to go first.

Ryan parked the bike along Colgate Street in Somers Point, and he rested his helmet on the back of the seat. He slowly walked up to the front door, and Joan opened the door before he had even had a chance to knock. She must have heard him pull up.

"Ryan! So nice to see you. I'm sorry. Were we supposed to be having dinner tonight?"

"No, no," Ryan answered as he wrapped his arms around her. "This is an unscheduled visit. Is that okay?"

"Of course, please come in," Joan answered as she led Ryan into the house.

"Is Russell around?"

"Yes. Let me go get him. Please, make yourself at home."

Ryan wandered around the living room looking at all of the pictures of Larkin and her parents and her sister. He loved coming here. He always felt so close to Larkin.

"Hi, Ryan. How are you?" Russell greeted him with an outstretched arm.

Ryan turned and shook his hand. "Hi, sir.

Good to see you." Ryan sat down on the couch next to Joan and across from Russell, who sat down in the recliner.

"I wanted to let you know that I am leaving town for a while."

Joan gasped, obviously surprised and confused. "Leaving town? Why? For how long?"

"A couple of weeks. Maybe less. Maybe more."

"Ryan, what's going on? Is everything okay?" Russell asked.

"Everything is okay. I just need to get away. There are too many things around here that remind me of Larkin. I can't seem to move on. I need to go somewhere where I can clear my head and not think about her all the time. I can't keep looking back into the past if I want to move forward."

"What about Lux? You seemed to really like her," asked Joan.

"I do. I do. But," Ryan paused, "but she deserves one hundred percent of my heart, and I can't give that to her."

"Well, you're not going to be able to give that to her unless you spend time with her," Joan said, pleading with Ryan.

Ryan reached out and grabbed her hand. "I know how much you really liked Lux. And I do too. I know what Larkin's letter said to you, and I know she wanted you to help me move forward, but I'm just not ready. It's not fair to Lux." Ryan knew that Larkin's parents weren't going to understand completely. He wanted to tell them about Larkin's visits and how she didn't come as often the more time he spent with Lux. But he knew that it would just complicate things, and he didn't want to upset them. "I really need to know that you are okay with me going away for a little bit. I need to know that you support me."

"Of course, we do," Russell said.

Ryan looked at Joan, and he could tell she was upset that he was leaving. "I just like having you around. I feel close to Larkin when you're here," Joan said.

"I'm coming back," Ryan assured her. "It's just for a few weeks. I promise. I didn't just want to bail and not say anything. I didn't want you to worry."

"Okay," Joan said. "But you need to promise that you will give Lux a chance when you get back."

"We'll see where my head and heart are at when I get back. Okay?"

"Okay," Joan replied hesitantly.

Ryan and Russell both stood up and shook hands. Joan walked Ryan to the door and hugged him before he walked out the door.

"Remember what Larkin said. She said by letting her love go, you'll be surrounded in it," Joan whispered in his ear.

Ryan nodded.

"Be careful."

"I will."

Ryan walked back to his bike, opened up his bag, pulled out a pen, and ripped out a piece of paper from his notebook. He met the tip of the pen to the paper.

Dear Larkin,

No more looking back.

All my love,

Ryan

Ryan folded the paper and placed it in the inside pocket of his jacket. He started up the engine and drove back to the middle of the Longport Bridge. He pulled over again and took out the letter. This time, instead of burning it, he ripped it up into tiny little pieces and let the wind carry it over the bay. Ryan turned the bike around and once again started his journey away from Longport, promising himself no more looking back. Not until he was ready to move forward.

CHAPTER 13

Riding his motorcycle out on the open road brought Ryan as much peace as when he was out on the water. He felt untouchable and out of reach. He didn't want to be around anyone right now so it was perfect. The temperature wasn't too warm or too cold. It was just right for an early autumn day. But as he sped across the Atlantic City Expressway, the winds occasionally picked up and bit at the part of his neck that was exposed to the air. Ryan maneuvered the Triumph in and out of traffic to a destination unknown. He would drive until he was tired, find a place to crash, and pick up where he had left off. He did plan to only be away for a couple of weeks, but he would stay away longer if he felt he needed to.

Ryan's brain was battered and bruised from all of the thoughts that were bouncing through his mind. His thoughts bounced back and forth between Larkin and Lux and all that had happened in the past three months. Memories of his visits with Larkin and the memories of the words they had written to each other coupled with the memories of the time he spent with Lux consumed his mind. His brain was tired, but he didn't know how to turn it off. He started to pretend that Larkin was riding on the back of the bike with her arms wrapped around his torso. He pretended that they were driving across the country together and that everything was back to normal. No sickness, no death, no letters, and no feelings for another woman. Just him and her and the world in front of them.

Ryan had wanted so badly for Larkin to be there with him. He got so lost in his make-believe thoughts that he swore he could actually feel her arms around him. He could feel her heart beating against him as she rested the side of her head against his back. It seemed so real. So real, that he actually reached his hand down to squeeze her hand that he had felt resting around his stomach. But what he had felt wasn't make-believe. It wasn't pretend. It was real and he had felt her squeeze his hand back.

"Larkin?" he cried out, slowing the speed of his bike down.

He could feel her breath against his neck. "Ryan, you have to go back. You have to go back now. Lux needs you. Turn around now."

"Larkin, what do you mean? Why?"

"Please, Ryan," she pleaded. "She needs you."

Ryan pulled over to the side of the road, but when he finally came to a complete stop, Larkin was gone. He frantically looked all around for her even though he knew he wouldn't find her. Her words were desperate. He could sense that she was worried, but he didn't understand why she had wanted him to go back. But he knew that he needed to. She wouldn't have come to him for no good reason. Larkin had been right about everything up until this point. Why would this time be different? Ryan put his helmet back on and hurried back home. He didn't know what he would be coming home to, but he had hoped Larkin would be there to guide him.

The closer Ryan got to Longport, the more he started to feel like something was very wrong. He was thankful he was on his motorcycle. He could get away with going faster a little bit easier. But no matter how fast he pushed that Triumph, he felt like his trip home was going in slow motion. Ryan didn't understand why Larkin kept telling him that Lux needed him. What could she possibly need him for? If anything, he was the one who needed help. What could he possibly do to help Lux? He couldn't even help himself.

Ryan was never happier to see the Longport Bridge. He sped across the bay into Longport and pulled the bike into his driveway. Ryan saw that Lux's car was in her driveway so he ran over to her house and rang the doorbell before frantically knocking when she didn't answer. He walked around her house to see if she was sitting on her back deck, and when he didn't see her there either, he started to become more and more concerned. He was worried that maybe something had happened to her inside the house so he started to look into the windows. He looked into each one starting from the front and working his way around the side before going back to the back deck. When he peered inside the deck's glass doors, he saw Lux's reflection from behind him. She was swimming in the inlet. He turned quickly around to watch her only to realize she wasn't swimming. She was drowning.

Ryan ran as fast as he could down the deck steps onto the beach. His body sliced through the water, and he could immediately feel the rip current tugging on his legs. Lux was about ten yards away to his left, and he let the current carry him to her. He could see that she was struggling to stay afloat, and he yelled out to her to stop swimming against the current. Lux tried to follow his directions, but she was no match for the violent rip tides. Ryan knew he needed to get to her faster so he dove his body under the water and let the current take him toward her. When his head broke the surface of the bay, he could see that Lux was no longer struggling and she was reaching out for him. He grabbed her hands and pulled her into him, and he guided her out of the water. He slowly sat her down onto the sand and cupped her face with his hands.

"Are you okay?"

Lux could barely catch her breath, but she was able to nod to let him know that she was going to be okay.

"What were you thinking? I told you not to go out into the inlet alone. Why would you do that?" Ryan was relieved that she was okay, but he couldn't keep his anger inside. Lux began to sob and he pulled her into his arms. "It's okay. It's going to be okay. I got you," Ryan assured her as he stroked the side of her head.

Lux finally caught her breath. "Ryan. I saw her," she said in between her gasps of air.

"Who?"

"Larkin. I saw her. She saved me. She pulled me to the top of the water."

Ryan was speechless. He couldn't believe what was happening. He held onto Lux as his eyes scanned the beach to see if he could see Larkin, but she was nowhere to be found. Ryan squeezed Lux tight as she continued to catch her breath.

"Come on. Let's go get you warm," Ryan said as he picked Lux up and carried her to the house. As he carried her, he continued to look around to see if he could see Larkin, but again, he wasn't able to find her.

Lux was curled up on her couch under several blankets, and Ryan was in her kitchen making her some hot tea. As he waited for it to finish, he was watching out the deck doors for any signs of Larkin. The squealing of the kettle quickly interrupted Ryan's concentration, and he proceeded to prepare Lux a cup of tea. He brought it in to the living room and handed it to her as he sat down next to her.

"Thank you," she quietly said.

Lux rested her head against the back of the couch, and Ryan reached out to grab her hand.

"Lux," he said before pausing. "Lux, what were you doing out there? Please tell me you weren't…—"

"No, Ryan. I wasn't."

Ryan knew Lux understood what he was trying to ask.

"I just wanted to be out in the water again. I wanted to feel that peace again. I wanted to be close to my brother. I would never try to take my own life."

Ryan knew exactly how Lux felt. He felt like that every day. But there was one difference. He had actually tried to take his own life. He hadn't wanted to admit it, but he knew it was time he did.

"I never told anyone this," he started, "but—" Ryan struggled to contain his emotions.

"It's okay," Lux interrupted, "you can tell me."

"Just before I met you," Ryan paused, "I wanted to drown. I tried to drown."

"What happened?" Lux asked.

"Larkin happened. She pulled me up to the surface." Lux squeezed Ryan's hand. "Since it happened, I never wanted to admit it. I made myself believe that I was diving into the water to be close to her. I swore I saw her reflection, and I went in to be with her. I thought she needed me to save her.

But deep down, I know she doesn't need to be saved. I do."

"We both do," said Lux.

"And it looks like she's saved us both," Ryan said.

"Can I ask you a question?" Lux asked.

Ryan nodded.

"I saw you leave on your motorcycle earlier. How did you know to come look for me?"

Ryan sighed and gave Lux a half-smile. "Larkin. She came and told me." They stared at each other speechless. It was hard to believe all that had just happened in the last few hours. And Ryan could tell that Lux was having a hard time making sense of everything. As much as he was concerned about her, he couldn't seem to forget about what she had said to him earlier this morning before she left.

"So, let me ask you something. Does this feel real to you? Did she feel real to you? Because it certainly feels real to me."

Lux was quiet for a moment.

"Ryan, I am sorry I said that she isn't real. I never wanted to make you think that I didn't believe you or that you are crazy. It's just that you had hurt me, and I wanted to hurt you back. I'm sorry."

Ryan knew Lux was sorry. And she was right. He had hurt her. The way he had treated her was unacceptable, and he felt pretty bad about it.

"I deserved it, Lux. And I'm the one who should be sorry. I never meant to hurt you."

"Then why did you? I don't understand."

"I guess I just want to be able to give you all of me, and not just part of me. You deserve more than that," Ryan tried to explain. He glanced over at her, and he could see the hurt in her eyes. It didn't matter what he would have said. Nothing would have made her feel better. So, all he could think of was to say he was sorry.

They sat in silence while Lux sipped her tea, and Ryan thought about all the events that had led up to this moment. All the things Larkin had been saying to him, and the dream he had been having. Everything was starting to fall into place. It's almost as if Larkin had sent Lux to him, not just for his sake, but for hers too.

"Lux, can you tell me what happened? What she did, what she said? Please?"

"I walked out until the water was at my knees. I wasn't going to go any further, but I was feeling unusually brave and decided that I was going to try to swim. I was doing okay for a while, but then I felt my body being pulled under. I couldn't fight it, and I was completely under the water. All the training in the world couldn't have prepared me for that. Everything turned dark, and I could start to feel myself fading away. I closed my eyes and tried to make peace with the fact that I was probably going to die. Suddenly, I felt my body being pulled up, and I opened my eyes. That's when

I saw her. She looked at me and smiled. And then she said, 'You're going to be okay. I got you.' She helped me to the top of the water, and I could see the worry in her eyes. Then she said, 'Please, don't give up on him.' And then there you were, seconds later."

Ryan fought the tears back. He didn't want Lux to see him cry. She reached out and grabbed his hand.

"Hey, I'm going to do what she asked of me. She saved my life, so it's the least I can do. I'm not going to give up on you. No matter how hard you push me away, I am going to be here for you, even if it is just as a friend. I won't give up on you. I'll help you through this. You shouldn't do it alone."

Ryan studied Lux as she pleaded with him. He couldn't understand how he had become so lucky to have met someone like her. No matter how many times he had pushed her away, she was always there waiting to help him. She was as stubborn as Larkin and that was what he needed. But it was more than that. It was a feeling he had when he was in her presence. It was the way he felt when she looked at him. And her beauty. He certainly couldn't deny her beauty. He had been denying all of these things but he decided he wasn't going to anymore.

"Lux, I don't think I can be friends with you," Ryan could see the disappointment and shock in her face. "I was going to go out of town for a couple of weeks. That was where I was headed today before I came back." Lux couldn't bear to look at him anymore. "The reason why I can't be friends with you is because," he paused, "because I am falling for you."

Lux quickly looked up and locked her eyes onto Ryan's, her lips hesitantly forming into a half-smile.

"I was thinking," Ryan continued, "of staying and maybe we can spend some time together and see what happens. What do you think?"

"I have wanted so badly to hear you say that to me," Lux paused for a moment, "but I don't know, Ryan. I'm afraid you're going to wake up one morning again and push me away because you're missing her. And I'm not saying that you can't miss her but—"

"Look," Ryan cut her off, "you're right. I am always going to miss her. But when I saw you drowning, and I was trying to get to you, all I could think of was how I couldn't lose you. I didn't think of her once. Just you. In that moment of panic and desperation, all I could think of was that I can't imagine continuing on without you. I need you, Lux. I didn't realize just how much until I thought I was losing you."

Lux threw herself into Ryan's arm. She wrapped her arms around his neck, and they held onto each other tighter than they ever had before.

"I need you too," Lux whispered in Ryan's ear.

As Ryan hugged Lux tight, he couldn't help but let his mind wander to Larkin, not because he needed her to be there, but because he knew that she was responsible for his relationship with Lux. She never gave up on pushing him toward Lux, and if it weren't for her warning, he would have never came and never realized how much he really did want to be with her. As happy as he was feeling in this moment, he also was feeling some sadness. He knew his time with Larkin was over. He knew she wouldn't come again. Ryan always thought that her letters were the best gift she could have ever given him. Today, he realized that he was wrong.

Larkin's best gift to him was Lux.

CHAPTER 14

The morning autumn sun broke through the thin bedroom curtains, and Ryan could feel the warmth of its rays on Lux's skin as he brushed her cheek with his thumb. His gentle touch pulled her eyes out from under their eyelids.

"Hi," she whispered.

"I'm sorry. I didn't mean to wake you," Ryan whispered back.

"It's okay."

The smile Lux greeted Ryan with was as beautiful as the sunrise, her whisper as soft as the warm summer wind. The past two weeks, Ryan had spent with Lux were more than he could have ever expected. More than he ever could have needed. He was falling hard for her, and he wanted to help her as much as she had helped him.

"I want to take you somewhere today."

"Where?" she softly asked, still waking up.

"It's a surprise. Are you up for it?"

Lux smiled and brushed her nose against his. "Sure. I'll go anywhere with you."

Ryan and Lux spent the morning having breakfast together and getting ready for the trip he was surprising her with. She kept pressing him about where he was taking her, but he wouldn't tell her. He was actually nervous about how she was going to react. All he could do was hope for the best, but prepare for the worst. Either way, he was going to be there for her and let her be what she needed to be.

Lux spent the majority of the trip trying to figure out where Ryan was taking her. As he continued driving north into New England, she kept guessing at potential destinations. Her first guess was spending the day in New York City. As he drove into Connecticut, she guessed maybe he was taking her to Boston. But when he crossed over the Massachusetts border into New Hampshire, he could see her excitement turn quickly into fear and hesitation.

"What are you doing, Ryan?"

Ryan knew Lux knew exactly where they were going. He didn't answer her question. He just smiled at her and kept driving.

"Ryan?"

Again, he smiled at her and kept driving.

"Ryan?" she asked again, this time with anger echoing through her voice.

Ryan knew he couldn't keep ignoring her.

"Lux, everything is going to be okay."

"Why are you doing this?"

"Look, I know what it is like to not want to be helped. But you never gave up on me and now I am happier than I have been in a long time. I just want to help you."

"This is different, Ryan. You know this is not the same as what you were dealing with. No one blamed you for Larkin's death."

Ryan pulled the car over and reached across the seat to grab Lux's hands. "Look, you have to talk to them. And if it doesn't go well, I will be here waiting. But if you don't do this, you will always wander, and you will always blame yourself. And that's not right. It wasn't your fault, Lux. I hate seeing you blame yourself."

Ryan reached up and wiped a single tear that escaped from Lux's eye. "Please, Lux, do it for me. I promise I won't let you fall."

Lux slowly nodded her head. "Okay. I'll try."

A half-hour later, Ryan pulled up to a rustic two-story log cabin surrounded by endless trees. There was a tire hanging from a large tree that was nestled off to the side of the house and a hammock tied between two trees that shaded the front of the house.

"Wow, nice place," Ryan said.

"How did you know where my parents lived

anyway?" Lux asked.

Ryan chuckled to himself. "Well, I kind of looked in your address book." Ryan glanced over at Lux. "Sorry. But I did owe you one."

Lux couldn't help but smile back. "I guess you're right."

Lux sighed and rested her head back onto the head rest. Ryan could see she was nervous. Her heart was practically beating out of her chest. He squeezed her hand.

"You can do this. Remember, I will be here waiting," he reassured her.

Lux hesitantly opened the car door, and before she stepped out, Ryan pulled her back in toward him and kissed her. "Take as long as you need. I brought something to read."

Ryan watched as Lux walked up to her parents' front door and knocked. He could see the shock and disbelief on her mother's face when she opened the door. Lux and her mother stared at each other for a moment before her mother opened the door to let her in.

Ryan settled in the driver's seat. He didn't know how long he would be waiting, but he would wait for as long as he needed. He wanted Lux to make amends with her parents. It wasn't right the way she felt about her brother's death. It wasn't her fault, and until she talked about it with them, she would always feel that it was.

Ryan wasn't exactly honest with Lux. He didn't bring something to read. Instead, he had brought a pen and paper so he could write. He never realized how easy it was to write his feelings down until the past couple of months. There was so much he wanted to say, and he knew he would be able to get it all out if he wrote it down instead of trying to say it. Writing to Larkin had become so easy and so healing. But this time, he wasn't writing to Larkin. He was going to write to Lux.

My dearest Lux,

I am a man who has loved and lost. I have loved so hard, it brought me to my knees. I have completely given myself to a woman that I thought I couldn't live without her. I thought it impossible to love another soul. But I now know that every decision I have ever made, every right, every wrong, every heartache, and every joy has led me to this exact moment in time. To the place where I am supposed to be. And that place is with you.

All I ask of you is to accept me as I am. As a man who will always love Larkin. Not a day will go by that I won't think of her, or miss her, or love her. Larkin has made me the man I am. She has shown me how to love to the depths of my soul, and without her, the man I am would not exist.

But I am also a man who is ready to share myself again. A man who is ready to show just how much I can love. For the past nine months, I haven't been able to catch my breath. I have been so overwhelmed with grief, I stopped looking forward and clung to the past. I stopped dreaming. And then you came along.

You are the day that keeps me breathing. You are the night that keeps me dreaming. You are the sun that keeps me warm, and the moon that lights my darkness. You are everything that I need, and everything that I want. When I look into your eyes, I see my future. I want to be your breath, your dream, your sun, and your moon. But most importantly, I want to be your tomorrow.

I didn't think I could ever love again. I couldn't have been more wrong.

I love you.

Ryan

Ryan folded the letter up and tucked it into his bag. It felt good to say that he loved her. And he did. He had fallen in love with her as fast and as hard as he had with Larkin. And he was finally happy again.

Two hours later, Ryan saw the front door open again. He saw Lux and her parents walk out onto the front porch. They exchanged words before Lux embraced each one of them. Her father kissed her on the forehead, and her mother had started to cry. He could tell they were tears of joy. He couldn't help but smile as he watched a big smile come across Lux's face. Halfway through Lux's walk back to the car, she turned to wave at them, and her parents' reciprocated. He noticed her parents' wave to him as he got out of the car to open her door. He waved back before guiding Lux into her seat.

Lux sat in silence for several minutes as Ryan started the drive back home. He glanced over at her a couple of times to make sure she was okay. She finally reached out and grabbed his hand.

"Thank you," she whispered.

"You're welcome," he said.

Ryan and Lux spent the six-hour ride home talking about her visit with her parents. They were happy to see her and had wanted to reach out to her, but they didn't know how. They had apologized for the way they had treated her, and they didn't blame her for what had happened to her brother. They were so inundated with grief that they had taken it out on her. Ryan could already see the change in Lux after talking with her parents. Her smile was brighter and her eyes were happier. She had told them about Ryan and all they had been through this past summer. They had wanted to meet him, but Lux wanted them to earn it. Not all was forgiven, but they were headed on the right track.

About a half-hour away from home, Ryan decided he wanted to give Lux the letter he had written.

"I have something for you. It's in my bag."

Lux reached inside the bag and saw the

letter with her name penned across the front. She looked at Ryan, and he could tell she was moved.

"You wrote one for me?" she asked.

"For you. Read it when you're ready. You don't have to right now, but when you're ready."

Lux immediately opened the letter and spent the next several minutes reading the words that Ryan had carefully wrote. He glanced over at her occasionally to see her reaction, and he could see her eyes filling with tears. It wasn't until the end when her smile lit up the dark night that had filled the car.

"I do, you know?" Ryan said after she finished folding the letter.

You do, what?"

"I love you." He smiled nervously as stared straight ahead, focusing on the road.

"I love you too," she said, moving closer to him so she could rest her head on his shoulder.

He kissed the top of her head and as he continued to focus on the road ahead of him, a shooting star caught his attention. He smiled to himself believing that it was Larkin smiling at him, letting him know she approved. Letting him know that she was happy.

The afternoon sun greeted Lux through her bedroom window while she sat on the edge of her bed, revisiting the letter that Ryan had written to her a couple of days ago. She couldn't believe how lucky she felt to have met someone like him—to have someone like him love her. She placed the letter down on the bed beside her and reached across to her nightstand. She picked up a picture of her and her brother that she had retrieved at her parents' house. She was so happy to have found this picture. It was her favorite one, but she had accidentally left home for Boston without it. As she studied the picture, she was amazed at how her emotions went from one extreme to another—from pure happiness to grief and sorrow. But she had to admit, since talking to her parents, her sorrow had eased enough that she could think about him without crying.

Lux was lost in a memory when Ryan walked into the room and wrapped his arm around her as he sat down beside her.

"You okay?" he asked.

Lux looked over at him and couldn't help but smile. His good looks alone were enough to make her smile. "Yes," she answered. How couldn't she be? she thought.

She saw Ryan notice the picture of her and her brother.

"He would have loved you." Lux laughed out loud. "*He* would have known who you were."

Ryan chuckled. "Well, if he was anything like you, I am sure I would have loved him too."

Ryan brushed a loose strand of Lux's hair behind her ear. "Do you remember when you asked me why I believed there is a heaven?"

"Yes, I do."

"Well, now you know. Larkin is the reason I believe. And I also believe that your brother is there too."

"Thank you. I believe he is too," Lux said.

"Are you ready to meet my friends?" Ryan asked, rubbing her shoulder.

Lux took a deep breath. "Yes, of course," she answered, shaking her head in disbelief.

"What?" Ryan asked.

"I don't know. I just still can't believe you're this movie star. You just don't seem like one. I mean, don't get me wrong. You *look* like one. But you don't really act like one."

"Well, what does one act like?

"Oh, I don't know."

"Cocky? Standoffish? Mean? Above everyone?" Ryan offered.

Lux shrugged her shoulders. "No, not necessarily. Please don't misunderstand me or think I am trying to judge you or your friends." Lux was concerned that maybe her intentions were coming across wrong.

"Oh, I don't. I know you. Well, there are many movie stars that fit that prototype, but I'm sorry to disappoint you. I think my friends might disappoint you too. We're nothing like that. We're the boring movie stars I guess," he said with a sarcastic smile.

Ryan took Lux's hand and led her out of the room, down the stairs, out the back deck, and across the beach to his place. Lux was nervous to meet Ryan's friends. She had learned about how close they were to Larkin, and Ryan had told her about Ian being the one to hold Larkin when she died. She knew she couldn't replace Larkin in their hearts. She didn't want to. She just wanted them to find a small corner for her to fit into.

Lux tried to hide her anxiety as Ryan introduced her to his best friends, Ian and his wife Linda, Justin and his wife Amanda, and Sarah. They were very welcoming, and they spent the afternoon talking, eating, drinking, playing card games, and roasting marshmallows. She had been able to spend a lot of time with the ladies when Ryan, Ian, and Justin would leave to throw a couple of rods in the bay. They had told her how lucky she was to have someone like Ryan, but at the same time, they were so happy that he was able to move on and find her. Sarah had shared in detail how low Ryan had been and how worried she was becoming about his well-being. Lux didn't realize until that night just how bad Ryan had been. She secretly vowed at that moment that she would never let him fall that low again.

Lux was especially happy when Ian pulled her aside and thanked her for making Ryan smile again. He had told her that he hadn't seen Ryan that happy since Larkin was healthy. Ryan's friends were as amazing as he had said they would be. Even in the company of strangers, Lux had never felt more at home.

Lux was sad to see Ryan's friends leave, but she was looking forward to having alone time with him. She was anxious to tell him how great his friends were. Ryan handed Lux a glass of wine, and they curled up on the couch in front of the fire. This had become her favorite time of the day. Resting the back of her head against his chest as his arms swallowed her body. Everything about him—his beauty, his scent, his voice, his touch—consumed her. She was the happiest she had ever been in her life, and she was going to do everything she could to make sure that would never change.

"So, what did you think of my friends?"

"Cocky. Standoffish. Mean. Above everyone," Lux answered, trying not to laugh.

"Oh, well, at least they didn't disappoint you," Ryan said with a chuckle.

"No, seriously, they were pretty great. Just like you. They were very welcoming, and they made me feel like I belonged."

"Well, you do belong. You belong with me."

Lux turned her head up toward Ryan and pressed her lips against his. She couldn't help but think about the conversation she had with Sarah about how grief-stricken he was. She wanted him to know that she would do anything she could to be what he needed.

"Hey, I want you to know that I am not going anywhere. I will never leave you alone, okay?" Lux assured him.

"Okay," he said.

"There was something I wanted to do tonight," Ryan said.

"What's that?" Lux was intrigued.

"I'll be right back."

Lux watched Ryan as he walked upstairs, and she waited and wandered what he was up to. She saw him come down with a stack of papers, and he sat down on the couch.

"What are those?"

"These are some of Larkin's letters. The ones that make me feel sad or angry. I'm ready to get rid of them."

"Are you sure?"

Ryan thought about it. "Yes. I'm sure. I still have the ones that make me feel happy. The ones that help me to remember how much I love her."

Lux watched as Ryan placed the letters into the fire. She could see a sense of peace come across his face as he watched them burn. She knew from that moment on that she would do everything she could to help him never lose that peace. Lux realized that this whole time she had been trying to replace Larkin, and there was no way she would ever be able to do that. She just needed to be Lux, and she was going to try the best that she could to help Ryan remember Larkin. Larkin was his past, and that past had made him the man he was today, and that was the man she had fallen in love with.

CHAPTER 15

Looking back. That was what Ryan had caught himself doing for the past ten months. He was always looking back to his life with Larkin.

The hot summer days were no longer, and the cool autumn breezes were now a daily occurrence along the Jersey coast. Boat traffic and beachgoers were far and few between as another summer had come to a close. The transition between summer and autumn was Ryan's favorite time of year. He liked the excitement of the Jersey Shore summers, but he loved the quietness that autumn had to offer. It had been two weeks since Larkin came to him on his motorcycle and warned him about Lux, and she hasn't come to see him since. He thought about her every day and wondered if he would see her again. He had written her one last letter, but he still hadn't burned it. He was having a hard time sending this one off.

The Saturday morning sun peeked through the slightly opened curtain in Ryan's bedroom, and the warm rays brushed upon his cheek. He rolled over to check the time and noticed his letter to Larkin sitting on the nightstand. Today was not going to be the typical Saturday for Ryan. No boat ride or fishing. No nighttime fishing next to the bonfire. Today, instead, he was going to burn that letter and begin to move on with his life. Without Larkin.

Ryan sat up in his bed and opened the letter. He wanted to make sure that what he had written was perfect—a perfect letter for his perfect Larkin.

My beautiful Larkin,

You know you love somebody when all you do is think of them. When all you do is imagine them next to you whenever they can't be there. When everything around reminds you of them. When everything you do, you do for them. But mostly, you know you love someone when you know you can't live without them.

For the past ten months since your death, all I have done is think of you and imagine you next to me with every move I make. These past ten months, all I have done, I've done for you. But mostly, these past ten months, I haven't wanted to live without you.

Since your death, I have looked for you amongst the shadows and amongst the stars, amongst the waves and the grains of sand. I have looked for you around every corner I turn and beyond every step I take. And you have been there with me this entire time. Not letting me fall and not letting me drown.

I know now, Larkin, who that faceless girl is in my dreams. The one next to you. The one you save. I know it is Lux, and I know that somehow you sent her to me. I don't know how, but I know you did. I also now know that the day on the water when you first came to me when I was drowning, I was trying to end my life. I didn't think I could live without you. But, my angel, somehow you knew I could.

Now it's Lux who I look for amongst the shadows and the stars, amongst the waves and the grains of sand. It's her who I look for around every corner I turn, and beyond every step I take. It's her who I imagine next to me with every move I make. And it's Lux who I now can't live without. But it is you, my sweet Larkin, who has kept me alive. It is you who has given me the strength to open my heart and love again. It is you who has taught me that life doesn't have to end when love does, but that love actually never ends, it transcends time and continues on forever, and you have to be strong to never let go of it. And I will never let go of the love I feel for you.

Please know, Larkin, that as I move on with my heart, I am not replacing you. I will always be there with you just as you are with me. Our love knew no bounds, and it will continue on forever amongst the shadows and the stars, and amongst the waves and the grains of sand.

> *My Love Always,*
>
> *Your Beautiful-Faced Boy*

As the warm sun slowly gave way to the twilight, Ryan ignited the bonfire. He didn't want to wait any longer to send the letter to Larkin. He was still hesitant to say good-bye, but he knew he needed to. He didn't think he would see her again, but still, he knew she was getting his letters. Ryan reached into his back pocket and grabbed the letter. He held it tight while he thought about all that had happened the past several months. He was a different man now. He had changed from a desperate and grieving loner to a strong and hopeful soul. He had Larkin to thank. She had guided him through that grief and led him to a safe place where he no longer would need her. That safe place was Lux. There was no question that he would always love Larkin. And his love for her taught him how to keep on loving.

For the last time, Ryan slowly placed the letter into the bonfire's flames and watched as his very last letter to Larkin dissolved into the moonlight. It was a perfect night—a perfect night to say good-bye to a grief-stricken past—but also a perfect night to say hello to a happy and peaceful future. As he watched the flames consume the paper, he felt as if a part of his heart was burning away too. A part of his heart that would be scarred forever, but strong enough to persevere through the pain. He felt sad and excited at the same time. Sad to say good-bye to the love of his life, but excited to say hello to love again. Tonight was the first time in a long while that he didn't feel alone.

The evening bay breeze grazed Ryan's face while he fed his old friends some bread as they circled overhead. They seemed to always be there at the time when he needed them most. They were there the day he started to read Larkin's first letter seven months ago, and now they were there when he was sending her his last.

The autumn moon was floating behind the clouds while Ryan prepped the bonfire, radio, and fishing rods for an evening to be spent with Lux. An evening of roasting marshmallows, slow dancing on the beach, and fishing. He was excited to see her. He felt like he was finally ready to give himself to her completely. He felt like he had a clean slate with nothing to hold him back. She deserved it. She had been there for him as he struggled to grieve. She had been patient and understanding. More importantly, she had given to him all of her, and he wanted to reciprocate. And ever since she had seen Larkin the day she nearly drowned, he felt more connected to her than ever.

Ryan anxiously waited for Lux's arrival and as he watched the tips of the flames melt into the atmosphere, a silhouette in the distance caught his attention. He would recognize that shadow anywhere. He watched as she moved along the edge of the water before stopping to gaze out into the ocean's distant horizon. He couldn't take his eyes off her, and he watched as she fed the seagulls a late night snack. A brush upon his shoulder startled him out of his trance, and he looked up to see Lux standing there. She was wearing a cream-colored sundress, and her hair was partially pulled back with gentle loose curls caressing the top of her sun-kissed shoulders. She was more beautiful than ever, he thought, and he was happy she had finally come.

"Hey, pretty girl, you finally made it," he greeted her as he took her hand and guided her to the chair next to him. Her smile was brighter than the stars, but her eyes were filled with concern, and he realized that she knew something was wrong. "Are you okay?" she asked as she rested her hand onto his knee.

He placed his hand on top of hers, and he smiled at her before looking off into the distance. He could feel the tears slowly building up in his eyes.

"She's here. Do you see her?" he asked, nodding into the direction of the silhouette he had just been watching.

After a quick glance over, Lux looked back at Ryan with sorrow in her eyes. "No," she said with regret in her voice. "I'm sorry, I don't."

Ryan had hoped that Lux could see her, but he wasn't surprised that she couldn't. Larkin had finally come back to see him and he knew why. She must have read his last letter. He knew what he needed to do, but he was terrified. He felt Lux squeeze his hand.

"Ryan, go see her. It's okay."

He turned to Lux as he squeezed her hand back, and when looked into her eyes, his fear began to diminish. Her smile, her beauty, her strength, and her understanding were everything he needed to get through this.

"I need to let her go," he said. "I am finally ready to let her go." He got up from his chair, and as he started to walk toward Larkin, he turned to look back at Lux.

"Thank you," he said.

"I'll be here waiting," she answered. "Take all the time you need."

Larkin turned toward Ryan as he approached her, and when their eyes met, he was overwhelmed by her presence. She was angelic, and her blue eyes glowed brighter than ever.

"My angel," he greeted her. "I didn't think I would see you again."

She smiled as she reached out to grab his outstretched hands. "I got your last letter. It was beautiful, Ryan."

Ryan broke their gaze and looked down trying to gather his thoughts. He felt sorry that he was saying good-bye to her. His sorrow overcame what little strength he had, and he couldn't fight the tears anymore.

"I am so sorry, Lark," he fought to say, still looking down.

Larkin quickly grabbed his face with her hands and brought his eyes back to hers.

"Oh, Ryan. Don't be sorry. This is what I wanted for you. Don't you see that?"

He saw tears building up in her eyes, and he knew it killed her to see him so sad. Deep down, he knew that she had been pushing him to love again.

"I will always love you," he said as he wiped away her tears. "More than anything."

"I know. I can feel it. It stayed with me." Larkin brushed a tear from Ryan's cheek. Ryan nodded as he struggled to let her go. "Will you dance with me?" he asked her.

Larkin smiled through her sadness, "Of course, I would love to."

Ryan led Larkin into a dance, and she rested her head onto his shoulder as their bodies swayed back and forth. "Thank you for saving her," he whispered as he gently rested his chin on her head. "Thank you for saving me."

Larkin looked up at Ryan and smiled. She studied him for a moment. "I want you to love her with everything you have. Love her the way you loved me. Love her with urgency. I want you to nurture that love, take care of it, and never let it go."

He nodded before she rested her head back onto his shoulder. He loved dancing with her. He loved feeling the weight of her head on his shoulder. He loved feeling her fingers interlocked with his. More importantly, he loved her more than anything. But he knew she was a ghost, and he couldn't continue to live his life this way. Ryan started to sing their wedding song, and Larkin laughed as he spun her around a few times before bringing her in close to him. They stared at each other for a moment before Larkin smiled and told him she loved him. He could feel her starting to pull away so he pulled her in to him again.

"One last kiss?" he asked.

Larkin smiled. "Of course."

Ryan grabbed her face, told her he loved her, and pressed his lips against hers. He let himself get lost in their kiss. It was as majestic a kiss that he had ever experienced, but it was also final. He knew it was the last time he was going to see her, so he put his heart and soul into it. And he would never forget the way it made him feel. As he released their embrace, he opened his eyes, and of course, she was gone.

"Good-bye, Lark," he whispered into the night air. He knew that was the last time they would walk the shoreline together.

Ryan gathered himself and started to walk back to the bonfire. He couldn't help but look back a couple of times to see if Larkin had come back, but he knew she wouldn't. He knew he would never see her again. He needed to somehow find the strength to stop looking back. As he got closer to the fire, he saw Lux still sitting there, waiting for him like she said she would. When she saw him, she got up from her chair and started to walk toward him. When they were close enough for their eyes to finally meet, he could see the worry in hers.

"Are you okay?" she asked.

He paused for a moment to study her and he couldn't help but smile. One look at her and he knew that he would never need to look back again. He was in love with this woman, and he knew that from here on out, everything was going to be okay. She made everything okay. She was the strength he had been looking for.

"I am now," he answered before lifting her up into his arms. She wrapped her legs around his waist and they embraced.

No more looking back.

About The Author

Jax Jillian was born in Albuquerque, NM but before she turned a year old, her parents moved east to Harrisburg, PA where she was raised. After graduating high school in 1995, Jax attended La Salle University (1999, B.A., Communication), Temple University (2001, M.Ed, Sport & Recreation Administration), and Central Pennsylvania College (2005, A.A.S, Physical Therapist Assistant).

She settled in Philadelphia, PA with her husband and son before she became a writer. Jax found a passion for motion pictures at a young age when she remembers "getting lost" in films, and that passion ultimately led her down the path to writing. She loves "getting lost" in her writing and particularly loves writing heartfelt love stories with a touch of tragedy which she believes is the key to truly reaching readers.

Jax is the author of Larkin's Letters and Ryan's Letters, two contemporary romance novels that have seen early success from reviewers, with both averaging 4.8/5 stars on Amazon and Goodreads. She is currently writing her third novel and aspires to write a screenplay one day.

When not writing, she works full time as a physical therapist assistant and as a mom to her three-year-old son.

Connect with Jax

Email mailto:jaxjillian@gmail.com

Website http://jaxjill.wordpress.com/

Twitter https://twitter.com/jaxjillian

Facebook http://www.facebook.com/JaxJillian

Amazon Author Page http://amazon.com/author/jaxjillian

Goodreads
https://www.goodreads.com/author/show/7089784.Jax_Jillian